Edward Fitzgerald

Edward Fitzgerald's Rubâ'iyât of Omar Khayyâm

Edward Fitzgerald

Edward Fitzgerald's Rubâ'iyât of Omar Khayyâm

ISBN/EAN: 9783337220051

Printed in Europe, USA, Canada, Australia, Japan

Cover: Foto ©Andreas Hilbeck / pixelio.de

More available books at **www.hansebooks.com**

EDWARD FITZGERALD'S

RUBÂ'IYÂT

OF

OMAR KHAYYÂM

WITH

THEIR ORIGINAL PERSIAN SOURCES

COLLATED FROM HIS OWN MSS., AND LITERALLY
TRANSLATED

BY

EDWARD HERON-ALLEN

LONDON
BERNARD QUARITCH
15 PICCADILLY, W.
1899.

PRINTED BY H. S. NICHOLS, LTD., 3 SOHO SQUARE, LONDON, W.

The decorations of this volume, other than those forming part of the original MS., are by Ella Hallward.

TABLE OF CONTENTS

PREFACE

THE object with which this volume has been
compiled has been to set at rest, once and for ever,
the vexed question of how far Edward FitzGerald's
incomparable poem may be regarded as a translation
of the Persian originals, how far as an adaptation, and
how far as an original work. In the Introduction to
my recently published translation of the Ouseley MS.
in the Bodleian Library at Oxford, and more particularly
in the Essay which terminates the second edition of
that work, I have dwelt at considerable length upon
the history of Edward FitzGerald's poem and the
influences of various Oriental works which are traceable
in it. As it is doubtful whether the present volume
will reach the hands of, or at any rate be critically
considered by, any students of the poem who have not
already had access to my former work, I do not think
that it would be either expedient or useful to repeat in
this place the information which is collected there,

but a short history of the major portion of Edward FitzGerald's material is necessary, for the purpose of showing why this question of translation, adaptation, or original composition should have been a question open to lengthy argument, and why it has been impossible to set it at rest until the present time, when forty years have elapsed since first Edward FitzGerald's poem attracted the attention of those great scholars and poets who rescued it, as recounted in the threadbare anecdote, from the oblivion of the penny box.

The influence of the Ouseley MS. upon the poem forms the subject of the volume to which I have referred, and, save in so far as it recurs in the parallels which give excuse for the present work, may be dismissed, but the doubts which have sprung up as to the extent to which Edward FitzGerald took, as his editor, Mr. Aldis Wright, says, "great liberties with the original," have arisen in consequence of the vicissitudes which have befallen the rest of the material from which the poet worked during the construction of his first edition. We have seen from Professor Cowell's letters to me (*loc. cit.,* p. xxxiii) that he made a copy of the Ouseley MS. for Edward FitzGerald just before he went to India in August, 1856. In another letter he says: "I got a copy made for him from the one MS. in the Bengal Asiatic Society's Library at Calcutta soon after I arrived in November, 1856. It reached FitzGerald June 14th, 1857, as I learn by a note in his writing. Some time after this I sent him a copy of that rare Calcutta printed edition which I got from my Munshi." To possess one-self therefore of full information as to what material Edward FitzGerald really worked from in making the original edition of his poem, it was necessary to consult, line by line, and word by word, the Calcutta MS. (noted as No. 1548 in the Bengal Asiatic Society's Library) and the Calcutta *printed* edition of 1836,—in addition, of course, to the Ouseley MS. Prof. Cowell most gener-ously placed at my disposal his copy of the Calcutta MS., but, as he himself has recorded (*loc. cit.*), the copy was made by an inferior scribe in a *nim-shikasta* hand which is exceedingly difficult to read. I therefore com-municated with Mr. A. T. Pringle, Director of Indian Records in the Home Department at Calcutta, himself a keen and critical student of Omar Khayyām, with a view to getting either a photographic reproduction, or a clean *nesta'lik* copy of this MS. made for me. Careful search and widely spread enquiry brought to light the fact that the MS. was lost, stolen, or strayed, so that Prof. Cowell's copy was the only record left of this portion of Edward FitzGerald's material. This copy I sent out to India, and had copied by a good writer, a copy being made at the same time to replace that which had been stolen.

I next addressed myself to the discovery of "that rare Calcutta *printed* edition," of whose existence, after searching in vain every European State library and many others, and every library in India of which I could learn, I began to have grave doubts, thinking that Prof. Cowell had inadvertently confused it with an edition *lithographed*, simultaneously at Calcutta and Teheran in 1836. In the summer, however, when I had given up all hope, one of Mr. Pringle's clerks picked up a copy of the long sought book in the Bazār at Calcutta, printed from type at Calcutta in 1836. A circumstance that greatly adds to the interest of this discovery, whilst at the same time it very greatly lessened my labours, lies in the fact that this edition is evidently printed from the lost Calcutta MS. itself, both introduction and quatrains being identical in readings and sequence. A few quatrains, including the repetitions, forming part of the MS. and nearly all those written in the margins of the MS. are omitted, but nearly all of these are added as an appendix to the book, the printer explaining in a short note that they were found in a *bayāz*, (or book of extracts) and were added in that place instead of in their *diwān* (or alphabetical) order on account of their more than ordinarily antinomian tendency. A very interesting question arises hereon, whether these latter were printed into the book from the margins of the MS. after being purposely or accidentally omitted, *or* whether they were written on to the margin of the MS. from this book at some date between 1836 and 1856. I think that the former is the more likely explanation, but in the absence of the MS. this question cannot be solved.

I find myself therefore in the interesting position of having the whole of FitzGerald's material before me; and though (so perfectly did Edward FitzGerald identify himself with his author's habit of mind) many other MSS. contain quatrains that closely resemble his marvellous paraphrase, there is nothing written by or attributed to Omar Khayyām which served FitzGerald for inspiration in making his first edition, other than what is to be found in the three, or rather two, texts above referred to. I have spoken already (and at length, in the Terminal Essay to my former volume) of the influences exerted by other Oriental poets upon his work, and especially that of the Mantik ut-tair, or Parliament of Birds of Ferid ud dīn Attār; where it was direct or exclusive I have set it down in the parallels which follow. The result of my observations may be summarised as follows:

Of Edward FitzGerald's quatrains, forty-nine are faithful and beautiful paraphrases of single quatrains to be found in the Ouseley or Calcutta MSS., or both.[1]

Forty-four are traceable to more than one quatrain, and may therefore may be termed the "composite" quatrains.

---

[1] The precise degree to which FitzGerald himself deemed it expedient to adhere to his original may be gathered by referring to quatrains of his which he has himself declared to be renderings of particular and isolated ruba'iyat. For example, those on pp. 14 and 15 of his Introduction and in the Notes to quatrains xviii. and xc. *Vide post:* pp 149 and 153.

Two are inspired by quatrains found by FitzGerald only in Nicolas' text.

Two are quatrains reflecting the whole spirit of the original poem.

Two are traceable exclusively to the influence of the Mantik ut-tair of Ferid ud dīn Attār.

Two quatrains primarily inspired by Omar were influenced by the Odes of Hafiz.

And three, which appeared only in the first and second editions and were afterwards suppressed by Edward FitzGerald himself, are not—so far as a careful search enables me to judge—attributable to any lines of the original texts. Other authors may have inspired them, but their identification is not useful in this case.

The "fillip," so to speak, given to FitzGerald's interest in the ruba'iyat, by the publication of Mons. J. B. Nicolas' text and translation of 464 "Les Quatrains de Khèyam" (Paris, 1867) must not be lost sight of, and may be held responsible for many, if not most of the variations and additions that differentiate the second, third, and fourth editions from the first. This volume, as FitzGerald himself records in his Introduction to the second and subsequent editions, "reminded him of several things and instructed him in others." Two of FitzGerald's later quatrains at least (Nos. 46 and 98) come from that text, and these I have never seen in any MS. text; and, in seeking the parallels to the present volume, I have collated exactly

5,235 ruba'iyat in the original Persian. I have appended
to every Persian ruba'i in the following pages, references
to the texts in which I have found the same ruba'i, in
the identical form, or more or less varied, and it will
be observed that, for the most part, the ruba'iyat which
inspired FitzGerald are those which have so appealed
to the Oriental mind as to be represented in nearly all
the MSS. and texts under examination. The Ouseley
MS. being the first text that occupied FitzGerald's
attention, where his inspirational lines occur both in
that MS. and the Calcutta MS., I have given the
Ouseley MS. version, noting any important variations
to be found in the Calcutta MS. It will be observed
that FitzGerald's tendency, after the second edition,
was to eliminate quatrains which were merely suggested
by the general tone and sentiment of the original poem,
and not the reflection or translation of particular and
identifiable ruba'iyat. The reader is especially recom-
mended, when studying these parallels, to turn to the
corresponding quatrain in the first edition, for Fitz-
Gerald often diverged further from the originals in
making his subsequent variations—notably, for instance,
in the first and forty-eighth quatrains.

With regard to my own translations of the originals
in the following pages, I may remark that the excessive
baldness of the translation is intentional, for I deemed
it better to put before the lovers of FitzGerald's poem
the closest and most unpolished English rendering,

rather than to attempt to clothe the literal meaning of the originals in graceful phraseology. The evils of such a course are abundantly displayed in Mr. Payne's recent translation founded upon the Lucknow edition.

In conclusion, I think that the dispassionate student of the following pages will allow me to claim that I have justified the opinion of FitzGerald's poem which I expressed in print a year ago: "A translation pure and simple it is *not*, but a translation in the most artistic sense of the term it undoubtedly is." But of Edward FitzGerald it may be said in the words of the Evangelist: "His foes have been they of his own household."

I desire to record in this place my most cordial thanks, for the invaluable assistance they have given me in the preparation of this volume, to Mr. A. T. Pringle, Professor E. B. Cowell, and Dr. E. Denison Ross, and to Mr. Aldis Wright, Edward FitzGerald's literary executor, and his publishers Messrs. Macmillan, for their very kind permission to reproduce in this volume the poem which has brought it into existence.

EDWARD HERON-ALLEN.

LONDON, *October*, 1898.

EXPLANATION OF THE REFERENCES IN THE
FOLLOWING PARALLELS

THE following are the alternative texts and translations referred to in the following parallels:—

O.—The Ouseley MS. No. 140 in the Bodleian Library at Oxford, dated A.H. 865 (A.D. 1460), containing 158 ruba'iyat. A facsimile and translation with notes, etc., were published by H. S. Nichols, Ltd. (London, 1898).

C.—The Calcutta MS. No. 1548 in the Bengal Asiatic Society's Library at Calcutta, containing 510 ruba'iyat. The original has been lost or stolen, but a copy has been made from the copy made for Edward FitzGerald at the instance of Prof. Cowell.

L.—The Lucknow lithograph. The edition referred to is that of A.H. 1312 (A.D. 1894), containing 770 ruba'iyat.

W.—The text and metrical translation published by E. H. Whinfield (London, Trübner, 1883), containing 500 ruba'iyat.

N.—The text and prose translation published by J. B. Nicolas (Paris, Imprimerie Impériale, 1867), containing 464 ruba'iyat.

S.P.—The text lithographed at St. Petersburg, A.H. 1308 (A.D. 1888), containing 453 ruba'iyat. Almost identical with N.

B.—A collection of poems lithographed at Bombay, A.H. 1297 (A.D. 1880), containing 756 ruba'iyat of Omar. Almost identical with L.

B. ii.—The MS. in the Public Library at Bankipur, dated A.H. 961-2 (A.D. 1553-4), containing 604 ruba'iyat.

P.—The MS. in the Bibliothèque Nationale, Paris. Supplément Persan, No. 823., ff. 92-113, dated A.H. 934 (A.D. 1527), containing 349 ruba'iyat.

P. ii.—Seven ruba'iyat written upon blank pages of a MS. of the Diwan of Emad. Dated A.H. 786 (A.D. 1384). Bibliothèque Nationale, Paris. Supplément Persan, No. 745. The handwriting is of the end of the 9th or beginning of the 10th century of the Hijrah.

P. iii.—Six ruba'iyat written in a handwriting of the 11th century of the Hijrah, on fol. 104 of a MS. collection of poems. Bibliothèque Nationale, Paris. Supplément Persan, No. 793.

P. iv.—The MS. in the Bibliothèque Nationale, Paris. Supplément Persan, No. 826, ff. 391-394. Dated A.H. 937 (A.D. 1530), containing 76 ruba'iyat.

P. v.—The MS. in the Bibliothèque Nationale, Paris. Ancien Fonds., No. 349, ff. 181-210. Dated A.H. 920 (A.D. 1514), containing 213 ruba'iyat.

T.—The MS. in the Library of the Nawab of Tonk. Apparently copied about A.D. 1840 principally from C., containing 369 ruba'iyat.

E.C.—The quatrains translated by Prof. E. B. Cowell in his article in the *Calcutta Review*, No. 59, March, 1858, p. 149.

De T.—The ten quatrains translated from the Ouseley MS. by Garcin de Tassy in his "Note sur les Ruba'iyat de 'Omar Khaïyām." (Paris, Imprimerie Impériale, 1857.)

V.—The metrical translation by John Payne, published by the Villon Society (London, 1898), containing 845 quatrains.

EDWARD FITZGERALD'S QUATRAINS.

I.

WAKE! For the Sun, who scatter'd into flight
The Stars before him from the Field of Night,
    Drives Night along with them from Heav'n, and
        strikes
The Sultān's Turret with a Shaft of Light.

THE PERSIAN ORIGINALS.

I.

THIS version of the opening quatrain is gradually evolved
through the four editions. The quatrain, which, in the first
edition runs:

> Awake! for Morning in the Bowl of Night
> Has flung the Stone that puts the Stars to Flight:
>   And lo! the Hunter of the East has caught
> The Sultān's Turret in a Noose of Light.

is inspired by C. 134.

C 134.   خورشید کمند صبح بر بام افکند

کی خسرو روز مهره در جام افکند

می خور که منادیِّ سحر گه خیزان

آوازهٔ اشربوا در ایّام افکند

> The Sun casts the noose of morning upon the roofs,
> Kai Khosrū of the day, he throws a stone into the bowl:
> Drink wine! for the Herald of the Dawn, rising up,
> Hurls into the days the cry of "Drink ye!"

II.

Before the phantom of False morning died,
Methought a Voice within the Tavern cried,
    "When all the Temple is prepared within,
"Why nods the drowsy Worshipper outside?"

Ref.:[1] L. 235. B. 232, C. 134, P. 320, T. 138—W. 233, V. 242.

It is not surprising that Mr. Aldis Wright, in his editorial note at the end of Messrs. Macmillan's definitive edition (London, 1890), states that "the first stanza is entirely his own," for, in this precise form the ruba'i is only to be found in the Calcutta MS. and in a recently discovered MS. copied largely from it and belonging to the Nawab of Tonk. The matter rests upon the word مهره (a stone) in the second line. مهره در جام افگندن means "to fling a stone into a cup or pot," which is the signal for "striking camp" among tribes of nomad Arabs. All the other texts I have seen read باده (wine) for مهره which has made the translators (Whinfield and Payne) properly render the passage "pours *wine* into the cup." The student is referred to the variations of this quatrain on p. 97 of Messrs. Macmillan's 1890 Edition.

II.

The inspiration for this quatrain is to be found in C. 5:

C 5. آمد سحري ندا ز ميخانه ما
کای رند خراباتي ديوانه ما
بر خيز که پر کنيم پيمانه ز مي
زان پيش که پر کند پيمانه ما

---

1 These references are to other MSS. and printed texts and translations in which the cited quatrain is represented. I say advisedly "represented," as the different texts differ a good deal. Often when a quatrain is repeated in the same text, variations may be found in it. The general scope of these variations may be appreciated by a glance at the notes to my translation of the Ouseley MS. (O.). I do not propose to deal with them here, excepting where there are important differences between the Calcutta MS. (C.) and the Ouseley, both of which were before Edward Fitz-Gerald and between which he had to choose.

III.

And, as the Cock crew, those who stood before
The Tavern shouted—"Open then the Door!
    "You know how little while we have to stay,
"And, once departed, may return no more."

There came one morning a cry from our tavern :
" Ho! our crazy, tavern-haunting profligate[1]
" Arise! that we may fill the measure with wine,
" Ere they fill up our measure (of life)."

Ref.: L. 1, B. 1, C. 5, B.ii. 1, T. 3—W. 1, N. 1, V. 1.

In FitzGerald's quatrain there is traceable the influence of one of the odes of Hafiz, translated by Prof. Cowell (in *Fraser's Magazine*, September, 1854), which he greatly admired. The lines in question run :

The morning dawns and the cloud has woven a canopy,
The morning draught, my friends, the morning draught !
It is strange that at such a season
They shut up the wine tavern ! Oh, hasten !
Have they still shut up the door of the tavern?
Open, oh thou Keeper of the Gates ![2]

the influence of these lines is carried on into the next quatrain.

————

III.

The inspiration for this quatrain is found in four ruba'iyat of the Calcutta MS.

C 641.   هنگام صبوح است وخروش ای ساقي
ما و مي و کوي ميفروش ای ساقي
چه جای صلحست خموش ای ساقي
بگذر ز حدیث و درد نوش ای ساقي

It is the hour for the morning draught, and the cock-crow, O Sāki,

————

1 *i.e.*, the Saki, or Cupbearer, or Drawer (generally a comely youth), to whom a large proportion of Omar's ruba'iyat are addressed.
2 Many parallels between these translations of Hafiz and FitzGerald's ruba'iyat may be found in the Terminal Essay to my former work.

Here are we, and the wine, and the street of the vintners,
O Sākī,
What time is this for devotions? Be silent, O Sākī,
Let be the traditions,[1] and drink to the dregs, O Sākī.

Ref.: L. 685, B. 676, C. 461, S. P. 448, B. ii. 599—W. 483, N. 454,
V. 737·.

C 207 ll 3 & 4.   مي بايد خورد و كام دل بايد راند

پيداست كه چند در جهان خواهي ماند

Thou must drink wine, and gratify the pleasures of thy
heart,
It is clear that so long (and no longer) thou wilt remain
in this world.

Ref.: L. 281, B. 277, C. 207—V. 285.

C 273.   وقت سحراست خيز اي مايهٔ ناز

نرمك نرمك باده خور چنك نواز

كاينها كه بخوابند نيابند بسي

و آنها كه شدند كسي نمي‌آيد باز

O, Essence of Delight! Arise, it is the dawn!
Softly, softly drink wine, and play the harp
For those who are asleep do not find much,
And none of those who are gone will ever come back.

Ref.: L. 431, B. 427, P. 289, C. 273, B. ii. 307, T. 173, P v. 163.—N. 235,
V. 469.

C 247.   وقت سحراست خيز اي طرفه پسر

پر بادهٔ لعل كن بلورين ساغر

كين يكدمه عاريت درين كنج فنا

بسيار بجوئي و نيابي ديگر

---

1 The *sunnat*, or Traditions of Muhammad, supplementing the Qur'ān,
and held in almost equal reverence.

IV.

Now the New Year reviving old Desires,
The thoughtful Soul to Solitude retires,
    Where the WHITE HAND OF MOSES on the
        Bough
Puts out, and Jesus from the Ground suspires.

It is the dawn ! Arise, oh strange boy !
Fill up the crystal cup with ruby wine.
For this moment (of existence) that is lent thee in this
    corner of mortality
Thou may'st seek long, but thou shalt not find it again.

Ref.: L. 402, B. 398, P. 224, S.P. 213, C. 247, B. ii. 282, P. iv. 21.—N. 214,
V. 425.

IV.

    This quatrain is translated from two ruba'iyat in the
Ouseley MS.

O 13. اكنون كه جهانرا بخوشي دست رميبست

هر زنده دلي را سوي صحرا هوميست

بر هــر شاخي طلوع موسي دستيست

در هر نفسي خروش عيسي نفسيست

Now that there is a possibility of happiness for the world,
Every living heart[1] has yearnings towards the desert,
Upon every bough is the appearance of Moses' hand,
In every breeze is the exhalation of Jesus' breath.[2]

Ref.: P. 194, O. 13—W. 116.

O 80. وقتست كه از صبا جهان آرايند

وز چشم سحاب چشمها بكشايند

موسي دستان ز شاخ كف بنمايند

عيسي نفسان زخاك بيرون آيند

Now is the time when by the spring breezes[3] the world
    is adorned,

---

1   *Zendha deli-ra* means the heart alive, or initiated in the spiritual
    sense, as opposed to the mere pleasure-seekers of the world.
2   See FitzGerald's notes to this quatrain.
3   C. reads " verdure."

V.

Iram indeed is gone with all his Rose,
And Jamshyd's Sev'n-ring'd Cup where no one
    knows;
    But still a Ruby kindles in the Vine,
And many a Garden by the Water blows.

VI.

And David's lips are lockt; but in divine
High-piping Pehlevi, with "Wine! Wine! Wine!
    "Red Wine!"—the Nightingale cries to the Rose
That sallow cheek of hers to 'incarnadine.

And in hope of rain it opens its eyes,[1]
The hands of Moses appear like froth upon the bough,
And the breath of Jesus comes forth from the earth.

Ref.: O. 80, L. 272, B. 268, C. 204, S.P. 186, P. 157—W. 201, N. 186, V. 276.

V.

This is a very composite quatrain, which cannot be claimed as a translation of all, or the main part of any of the C. or O. quatrains. All the texts, as indeed all Persian poetry, is filled with references of which we find an echo here. In the authorities at our disposal, Jamshyd is referred to in C. 254. The Ruby in the Wine occurs in O. 39, 87, 149, and in C. 296, 304, 413, and 460. The Garden by the Water occurs in O. 151 (C. 415), and in C. 44 and 417. I have never found any reference to the Garden of Iram in quatrains attributed to Omar Khayyām.[2]

VI.

This quatrain (eliminating the reference to David[3]) is translated from

O 67. روزیست خوش وهوا نه گرمست نه سرد

ابر از رخ گلزار همی شوید گرد

بلبل بزبان پهلوی با گل زرد

فریاد همی زند که می باید خورد

It is a pleasant day, and the weather is neither hot nor cold;

---

1 C. reads " In the eyes of the clouds the veils are parted."
2 See the Terminal Essay above referred to.
3 The sweet voice of David recurs continually in Persian poetry. We find it in C. 89 *et passim*.

VII.

Come, fill the Cup, and in the fire of Spring
Your Winter-garment of Repentance fling :
  The Bird of Time has but a little way
To flutter—and the Bird is on the Wing.

The rain has washed the dust from the faces of the
    roses ;
The nightingale in the Pehlevi tongue[1] to the yellow[2]
    rose
Cries ever : "Thou must drink wine ! "

Ref. : O. 67, L. 291, B. 287, SP. 153, P. 230—W. 174, N. 153, V. 294.

VII.

This is another composite quatrain, and the similarity of
its sentiment to that of No. 94 (*post*) makes it somewhat
difficult to allocate the parallels to it. The two first lines
come from two quatrains in C.

C 431.   هر روز برآنم که کنم شب توبه

از جام وپیاله‌ٔ لبالب توبه

اکنون که رسید وقت گل هر غم نیست

در موسم گل ز توبه یا رب توبه

Every day I resolve to repent in the evening,
Repenting of the brimful goblet, and the cup;
(But) now that the season of roses has come, I cannot
    grieve,
Give penitence for repentance[3] in the season of roses,
    O Lord !

Ref. : C. 431, L. 655, B. 647, B. ii. 510—W. 425, V. 704,

C 460 ll 1 & 2.   بشکفت شگوفه می‌بیار ای ساقی

دست از عمل زهد بدار ای ساقی

---

1 Pehlevi was the language of the ancient Persians of pre-Muham-
    madan times. FitzGerald's description of it as "old heroic
    Sanskrit " is erroneous.

2 Yellow is the colour indicative in Persian literature of sickness or
    misery, corresponding to our word " sallow."

3 *i.e.*, " permit us to regret our repentance."

VIII.*

Whether at Naishápúr or Babylon,
Whether the Cup with sweet or bitter run,
    The Wine of Life keeps oozing drop by drop,
The Leaves of Life keep falling one by one.

---

* Numbers of quatrains distinguished by the asterisk indicate that the quatrains were not in FitzGerald's first edition, but made their appearance in the second or subsequent editions. FitzGerald may therefore have been "reminded of" them by (and in some instances took them direct from) the text and translation of Nicolas, referred to as N.

The flowers are blooming, bring wine, O Sākī,
Abandon the practices of the zealot, O Sākī.

Ref.: C. 460, L. 684, B. 675, B. ii. 540—V. 736.

The image of the flight of time permeates the whole of
the quatrains. The precise image that FitzGerald uses in
ll. 3 and 4 I find in the 24th distich of the Mantik ut-tair
of Ferid ud-dīn Attār :—

مرغ گردون در رهش پر مي زند

The bird of the sky flutters along its appointed path.

VIII.*

This quatrain is taken mainly from O. 47 (C. 123). It
does not occur in the first edition, and FitzGerald was
evidently "reminded of it" by Nicolas, in whose reading of
the text, alone, the town of Naishapur is mentioned instead of
Balkh. Balkh and Babylon are constantly interchanged in
Persian *belles lettres.*

O 47. چون عمر همي رود چه بغداد وچه بلخ

پيمانه چو پر شود چه شيران وچه تلخ

مي خور که پس ازمن وتو اين ماه بسي

از سلخ بغره آيد از غره به سلخ

Since life passes; what is Baghdad and what is Balkh?
When the cup is full, what matter if it be sweet or
bitter?[1]
Drink wine, for often, after thee and me, this moon
Will pass on from the last day of the month to the first,
and from the first to the last.

---

1 C. reads " Since life passes, what is sweet and what is bitter ? "

IX.

Each Morn a thousand Roses brings, you say;
Yes, but where leaves the Rose of Yesterday?
    And this first Summer month that brings the
        Prose
Shall take Jamshyd and Kaikobád away.

Ref.: O. 47, L. 229, B. 226, C. 123, S.P. 105, P. 51, T. 99—W. 134, N. 105, E.C. 2, V. 236.

If closer reference for line 3 be required, it may be found in N. 18, ll. 3 and 4.

N 18 ll 3 & 4. هم ساقي ماحاق صراحي در دست

هم بر لب ساغر آمده جان شراب

Whether our Sākī holds the neck of the bottle in his hand,
Or the soul of wine oozes over the rim of the cup.

Ref.: L. 35, B. 32, S.P. 18.—W. 21, N. 18, V. 33.

" The leaves of life " recur constantly either as leaves of a tree, or of a book. FitzGerald's inspiration comes from C. 377, ll. 1 and 2. (*Vide* also *sub.* No. 9.)

C 377 ll 1 & 2. آن لعظه که از اجل گریزان گردم

چون برگ رزان ز شاخ ریزان گردم

At the moment when I flee from destiny,
And fall like the leaf of the vine, from the branch.

Ref.: C. 377, L. 574, B. 567, S.P. 265, B. ii. 353, T. 249.—W. 309, N. 266, V. 614.

IX.

This quatrain owes its origin to three separate ruba'iyat, viz. :—

O 135 ll 3 & 4. در سایهٔ گل نشین که بس گل که زیاد

در خاك فرو رفته وبا خاك شده

Sit in the shade of the rose, for, by the wind, many
    roses
Have been scattered to earth and have become dust.

Ref.: O. 135, L. 671, B. 663, S.P. 366, B.ii. 483, T. 277—W. 414, N. 370, V. 720.

X.

Well, let it take them! What have we to do
With Kaikobád the Great, or Kaikhosrú?
Let Zál* and Rustum bluster as they will,
Or Hátim call to supper—heed not you.

---

* It will be observed that the introduction of Zal in this
line was made by FitzGerald in the third edition for metrical
effect. The versions in the first edition " Let Rustum lay about
him as he will," and in the second "Let Rustum cry ' to battle '
as he likes," are closer to the phrase in the original " Rustum
son of Zal."

C 500 ll 1 & 2.   از آمدن بهار و از رفتن دی

اوراق وجود ما همیگردد طی

By the coming of Spring and the return of December[1]
The leaves of our life are continually folded.

Ref.: C. 500, L. 745, B. 731, P. 242, S.P. 397 B. ii. 531—W. 444, N. 402,
V. 797.

C 481 ll 3 & 4.   کافگندبهاك صد هزاران جم و کی

این آمدن تیر مه و رفتن دی

For it has flung to earth a hundred thousand Jams
and Kais,[2]

This coming of the first - summer - month and departing
of the month December.

Ref.: C. 481, L. 712, B. 701, S.P. 449, P. 216, B.ii. 603—W. 484, N. 455,
V. 764.

X.

The first two lines of this quatrain echo two fragments
from the MSS.

O 139 ll 3 & 4.   جامیش به از ملك فریدون صد بار

خشت مسرغم زتاج کیخسرو به

The cup is a hundred times better than the kingdom of
Ferīdūn,[3]
The tile that covers the jar is better than the crown of
Kai Khosrū.

Ref.: O. 139, L. 650, B. 642, S. P. 378, P. 246, B. ii. 511, P. v. 178—N. 382,
V. 699.

-----

1 *Dai* is the month that ushers in the winter quarter of the Muhammadan year.

2 *i.e.*, Jamshyd the " Roi soleil " of early Persian history, and the
Kaianian dynasty—Kai Kobâd, Kai Kawūs, Kai Khosrū, etc."

3 Ferīdûn was the sixth king of the Paish-dadian dynasty. *Jāmish* is
evidently an error for *Jām-ist*. *Vide* the MS.

XI.

With me along the strip of Herbage strown
That just divides the desert from the sown,
    Where name of Slave and Sultán is forgot—
And Peace to Mahmúd on his golden Throne!

XII.

A Book of Verses underneath the Bough,
A Jug of Wine, a Loaf of Bread—and Thou
    Beside me singing in the Wilderness—
Oh, Wilderness were Paradise enow!

C 57 ll 1 & 2. یكچرعہ مي ز ملك كاوس بہست

وز تخت قباد و ملكت طوس ابہست

One draught of wine is better than the Empire of Kawūs,
And is better than the Throne of Kobād and the Empire
of Tūs.

Ref.: C. 57, L. 122, B. 119, S. P. 61. P. 297—W. 64, N. 61, V. 121.

The last two lines are translated from

C 503 ll 3 & 4. گردن منہ ار خصم بود رستم زال

منت مبر ار دوست بود حاتم طي

Bow not thy neck though Rustum son of Zāl be thy foe,
Be not grateful though Hātim Tai befriend thee.[1]

Ref.: C. 503, L. 746, B. 732, S. P. 411, P. 150, B. ii. 552, P. iv. 23—
W. 455, N. 416, V. 798.

XI. & XII.

This pair of quatrains must be considered together.
They owe their origin to the following:

O 155. گر دست دھد زمغز گندم نانی

از مي کدوي ز گوسفندي رانی

وانگه من وتو نشستہ در ویرانی

عیشي بود آن لہ خد ھر سلطانی

If a loaf of wheaten bread be forthcoming,
A gourd of wine, and a thigh-bone of mutton,
And then, if thou and I be sitting in the wilderness,—
That were a joy not within the power of any Sultan.

Ref.: O. 155, C. 474, L. 697, B. 688, S.P. 442, P. 229, B. ii. 591, T. 2 92,
P. iv. 24, P. v. 109—W. 479, N. 448, V. 749.

---

1 See FitzGerald's note to this quatrain.

XIII.

Some for the Glories of This World; and some
Sigh for the Prophet's Paradise to come;
    Ah, take the Cash, and let the Credit go
Nor heed the rumble of a distant Drum!

O 149.

لنگي مي° لعل خواهم و ديواني

مدّ رمقي بـايد و نصف نـاني

وانگه من وتو نشسته در ويراني

خـوشتر بـود از مملكت سلطاني

I desire a flask of ruby wine and a book of verses
Just enough to keep me alive,[1] and half a loaf is needful,
And then, that thou and I should sit in the wilderness,
Is better than the kingdom of a Sultan.

Ref.: O. 149, S.P. 408.—W. 452, N. 413, E.C. 13.

XIII.

The original of this quatrain is found in

O 34.

گويند بهشت عدن باحور خوشست

من مي گويم كه آب الگور خوشست

اين نقد بگير و دست ازان نسيه بدار

كـاواز دهل برادر از دور خوشست

They say that the Garden of Eden is pleasant with houris:
I say that the juice of the grape is pleasant.
Hold fast this cash and keep thy hand from that credit,
For the noise of drums, brother, is pleasant from afar.

Ref.: O. 34, C. 51, L. 95, B. 91, P. iii. 3, P. 323, P. v. 36.—W. 108, V. 95.

C. 156 is almost identical in sentiment :—

C 156.

گويند بهشت و حوض كوثر باشد

آنجا مي ناب و مهد و شكّر باشد

پر كن قدح باده وبر دست نه

نقدي ز هزار نسيه بهتر باشد

---

1 Literally " a stopper of the last breath."

They say that there will be heaven and the Fount of
    Kausar,[1]
That there, there will be pure wine and honey and sugar,
Fill up the wine-cup and place it in my hand,
(For) ready cash is better than a thousand credits.

Ref.: C. 156, L. 297, B. 293, S. P. 169, B.ii. 223, T. 141—N. 169, V. 300.

C. 288 reproduces the same image, and we have a parallel
for ll. 1 and 2 in ll. 1 and 2 of C. 225.

C 225 ll 1 & 2.   قومي ز خيال, در غرور افتادند

و اندر طلب حور و قصور افتادند

Mankind are fallen from vain imagining into pride,
And are consumed in the search after houris and palaces.[2]

Ref.: C. 225, L. 279, B. 275, S.P. 167, T. 163—W. 184, N. 167, V. 283.

O. 40 may also be cited for the closeness of its parallel
both to this, and to the preceeding quatrain :

O 40.   من هیچ ندانم که مرا آنکه سرشت

از اهل بهشت گفت یا دوزخ زشت

قــولي وبتي وبادة بـرلب كشـت

این هرسه مرا نقد ولرا نسیه بهشت

I know not whether he who fashioned me
Appointed me to dwell in heaven or in dreadful hell

---

1 Kausar, in Persian mythology, is the head-stream of the Muhammadan Paradise, whence all other rivers are supposed to flow. A
whole chapter of the Qur'ān is devoted to this miraculous stream,
whose Sākī is Alī, the son-in-law of Muhammad.

2 This word قصور is a quotation from a famous verse in the Qur'an,
xxv. 11. " Blessed is He who, if He pleaseth, will make for thee
a better provision than this, namely, gardens under which rivers
flow, and he will provide thee palaces."—E. B. C.

XIV.

Look to the blowing Rose about us—" Lo,
" Laughing,' she says, " into the world I blow,
    " At once the silken tassel of my Purse
" Tear, and its Treasure on the Garden throw."

XV.

And those who husbanded the Golden grain,
And those who flung it to the winds like Rain,
    Alike to no such aureate Earth are turn'd
As, buried once, Men want dug up again.

(But) some food, and an adored one, and wine[1] upon the
  green bank of a field—
All these three are present cash to me : thine be the
  promised heaven !

Ref. : O. 40, L. 89, B. 85, C. 107, S. P. 92, T. 84, P. v. 176—W. 94,
N. 92, V. 89.

XIV.

This quatrain is translated from C. 383.

C 383. گل گفت که دست زر فشان آوردم

خندان خندان سر بجهان آوردم

بند از سر کیسه بر گرفتم رفتم

هر نقد که بود در میان آوردم

The rose said : I brought a gold-scattering hand,
Laughing, laughing, have I blown into the world,
I snatched the noose-string from off the head of my
  purse and I am gone !
I flung into the world all the ready money that I had.

Ref. : C. 383 *only*.

XV.

The inspiration for this quatrain comes from O. 68.

O 68. زان پیش که بر سرت شبیخون آرند

فرمای که تا باده گلگون آرند

تو زر نه ای غافل نادان که ترا

در خاک نهند وباز بیرون آرند

Ere that fate makes an attack upon thy head
Give orders that they bring thee rose-coloured wine;

---

1   C. reads for "food" and "wine," "goblet" and "lute," whence we get
    "thou beside me *singing* in the wilderness."

XVI.

The Worldly Hope men set their Hearts upon
Turns Ashes—or it prospers; and anon,
    Like Snow upon the Desert's dusty Face,
Lighting a little hour or two—is gone.

XVII.

Think, in this batter'd Caravanserai
Whose Portals are alternate Night and Day,
    How Sultán after Sultán with his Pomp
Abode his destined Hour, and went his way.

Thou art not treasure, O, heedless dunce! that thee
They hide in the earth and then dig up again. [1]

Ref.: O. 68, C. 151, L. 277, B. 273, S.P. 156, P. 336, Pv. 11—W. 175,
N. 156, E.C. 31, V. 281.

XVI.

The inspiration for this quatrain is to be found in C. 266.

C 266. ‏ای دل همه اسباب جهان ساخته گیر‏
‏دنیا همه سر بسر ترا خواسته گیر‏
‏و انگاه بروی آن چو در صحرا برف‏
‏روز دو سه نشسته و بر خاسته گیر‏

O heart! suppose all this world's affairs were within
your power,
And the whole world from end to end as you desire it,
And then, like snow in the desert, upon its surface
Resting for two or three days, understand yourself to be
gone!

Ref.: C. 266, L. 420, B. 416, P. 144, B. ii. 260, T. 168—V. 443.

XVII.

This quatrain owes its origin to C. 95.

C 95. ‏این کهنه رباطرا که عالم نامست‏
‏آرامگه ابلق صبح وشام امست‏
‏بزمیست که واماندهٔ صد جمشید امست‏
‏قصر یست که تکیه گه صد بهرامست‏

---

1 These two lines refer to the practice in the East of burying treasure
to hide it when a night attack (line 1) of dacoits or robbers is
anticipated.

XVIII.

They say the Lion and the Lizard keep
The Courts where Jamshyd gloried and drank deep:
    And Bahrām, that great Hunter—the Wild Ass
Stamps o'er his Head, but cannot break his Sleep.

XIX.

I sometimes think that never blows so red
The Rose as where some buried Cæsar bled;
    That every Hyacinth the Garden wears
Dropt in her Lap from some once lovely Head.

This worn caravanserai which is called the world
Is the resting-place of the piebald horse of night and
　　day;
It is a pavilion which has been abandoned by an
　　hundred Jamshyds;
It is a palace that is the resting-place of an hundred
　　Bahrāms.[1]

Ref.: C. 95, L. 203, B. 200, S. P. 67, P. 120, B. ii. 42, T. 79 and 357—
W. 70, N. 67, V. 199.

XVIII.

The original of this quatrain is C. 99.

C 99.　ان قصر که بهرام در و جام گرفت
روبه بچه کرد و شیر آرام گرفت
بهرام که گور میگرفتی دایم
امروز نگر که گور بهرام گرفت

In that palace where Bahrām grasped the wine-cup;
The foxes whelp, and the lions take their rest;
Bahrām who was always catching (*gūr*) wild asses,—
To-day behold that the (*gūr*) grave has caught Bahrām.

Ref.: C. 99, L. 210, B. 207, S.P. 69, P. 48 and 139, B.ii. 51, T. 82 and
294, P.iv. 12, P.v. 156—W. 72, N. 69, V. 205.

XIX.

The original of this quatrain is:

O 43.　هر جا که گلی ولاله زاری بودمست
از سرخی خون شهریاری بودمست
هر شاخ بنفشه کز زمین می روید
خالیست که بر رخ نگاری بودمست

1　See FitzGerald's note upon this hero, and the following quatrain.

3

XX.

And this reviving Herb whose tender Green
Fledges the River-lip on which we lean—
    Ah, lean upon it lightly! for who knows
From what once lovely Lip it springs unseen!

XXI.

Ah, my Belovéd fill the Cup that clears
To-DAY of past Regrets and future Fears:
    To-morrow!—Why, To-morrow I may be
Myself with Yesterday's Sev'n thousand Years.

Everywhere that there has been a rose or tulip bed,
It has come from the redness of the blood of a king;
Every violet shoot that grows from the earth
Is a mole[1] that was (once) upon the cheek of a beauty.

Ref.: O. 43, C. 47, L. 110, B. 106, B. ii. 105, T. 304, P. v. 159.—W. 104,
E.C. 4, V. 109.

XX.

The original of this quatrain was

C 44. هر سبزه که درکنار جوئي رستست
گوئي ز لب فرشته خوئي رستست
هان بر سر سبزه پا بخواري ننهي
کان سبزه ز خاك لاله روئي رستست

All verdure that grows upon the margin of a stream,
You may say, grows from the lip of one angel-natured;
Beware not to set foot contemptuously upon the verdure,
For that verdure grows from the clay of one tulip-cheeked.

Ref.: C. 44, L. 62, B. 59, S.P. 59, P. 64, T. 349, P. iv. 20.—W. 62,
N. 59, V. 61.

XXI.

This quatrain is translated from C. 348.

C 348. اي دوست بیا تا غم فردا نخوریم
وین یکدمه نقدرا غنیمت شمریم
فردا که از ین روي زمین در گذریم
با هفتهزار سالگان سر بسریم

---

1 Moles or " beauty spots " are very highly esteemed in the East.

XXII.

For some we loved, the loveliest and the best
That from his Vintage rolling Time hath prest,
    Have drunk their Cup a Round or two before,
And one by one crept silently to rest.

XXIII.

And we, that now make merry in the Room
They left, and Summer dresses in new bloom,
    Ourselves must we beneath the Couch of Earth
Descend—ourselves to make a Couch—for whom?

Come, O friend! and let us not suffer anguish con-
    cerning the morrow,
Let us take advantage of these few ready-money
    moments,
When, to-morrow, we depart from the face of the earth
We shall be equal with those who went seven thousand
    years ago.

Ref. C. 348, L. 546, B. 540, S.P. 268, P. 122, B.ii. 351, T. 233, P.v. 96
—W. 312, N. 269, V. 586.

XXII.

The inspiration for this quatrain is found in C. 185.

C 188.   یاران موافق همه از دست شدند
در پای اجل یکان یکان پست شدند
بودند بیک شراب در مجلس عمر
دَوْری دو ز ما پیشترک مست شدند

All my sympathetic friends have left me,
One by one they have sunk low at the foot of Death.
In the fellowship of souls they were cup-companions,
A turn or two before me they became drunk.

Ref.: C. 185, L. 381, B. 377, P. ii. 4, B. ii. 141—W. 219, V. 379.

XXIII.

The main inspiration of this quatrain comes from

C 388.   بر خیز و مخور غم جهان گذران
بنشین و جهان بشادکامی گذران
در طبع جهان اگر وفائی بودی
نوبت بتو خود نیامدی از دگران

Arise, and do not sorrow for this fleeting world,
Be at peace, and pass through the world with happiness.
If the nature of the world were constant
The turn of others would not have descended to you
yourself.[1]

Ref.: C. 388, L. 585, B. 578, S. P. 322, P. 159 and 178, B. ii. 430, T. 264,
P. iv. 29 and 62—W. 366, N. 325, V. 632.

Combined with the suggestion contained in this ruba'i,
we find the echo of a sentiment that recurs continually in
the originals, *e.g.*:

C 82 ll 3 & 4.   این سبزه که امروز تماشاگه ماست
تا سبزهٔ خاك ما تماشاگه کیست

This verdure, which for the present is my pleasure-
ground
Until the verdure (springing) from my clay shall become
a pleasure-ground—for whom ?

Ref.: C. 82, L. 191, B. 188, S. P. 70, P. 305, B. ii. 36, T. 63 and 351—
W. 73, N. 70, V. 187.

O 129 ll 3 & 4.   بر سبزه نشین بتا که بس دیر نماند
تا سبزه برون دمد زخاك من وتو

Sit upon the greensward, O Idol, for it will not be long
Ere that greensward shall grow from my dust and thine.

Ref.: O. 129, C. 416, L. 634, B. 626, S. P. 345, P. 47, B. ii. 464, P. v. 131
—W. 390, N. 348, E. C. 3, V. 683.

---

1 *i.e.*, If life were eternal, you could not take the place of others who
    have died before you. L. 2, *lit.*: "let the world pass, &c."

XXIV.

Ah, make the most of what we yet may spend,
Before we too into the Dust descend;
   Dust into Dust, and under Dust to lie,
Sans Wine, sans Song, sans Singer, and—sans End!

XXV.

Alike for those who for To-DAY prepare,
And those that after some To-MORROW stare,
   A Muezzin from the Tower of Darkness cries,
"Fools! your Reward is neither Here nor There."

XXIV.

The inspiration for this quatrain is found in the following:

O 76. مگذار که غصّه در کنارت گیرد

واندوه محال روزگارت گیرد

مگذار کتاب ولب یار ولب کشت

زان پیش که خاك درکنارت گیرد

Do not allow sorrow to embrace thee,
Nor an idle grief to occupy thy days,
Forsake not the book and the lover's lips and the green
    bank of the field,
Ere that the earth enfold thee in its bosom.

Ref.: O. 76, C. 173, L. 315. B. 311, P. 189, B. ii. 233, T. 121, P. v. 39—
de T. 9, V. 317.

O 35. می خور که بزیر گِل بسی خواهی خفت

بی مونس وبی حریف وبی همدم وجفت

Drink wine, for thou wilt sleep long beneath the clay
Without an intimate, a friend, a comrade, or a mate.

Ref.: O. 35, C. 80, L. 188, B. 185, P. 284, T. 60—W. 107, V. 184.

XXV.

The inspiration for this quatrain is in

C 396. قو می متفکّرند درملهب و دین

جمعی متحیّرند در شك و یقین

ناگاه منادئی بر آید ز کمین

كای بیخبران راه نه آنست و نه این

XXVI.

Why, all the Saints and Sages who discuss'd
Of the Two Worlds so wisely—they are thrust
    Like foolish Prophets forth; their Words to scorn
Are scatter'd, and their Mouths are stopt with dust.

Some are immersed in contemplation of doctrine and faith,
Others stand stupefied between doubt and certainty,
Suddenly a Muezzin, from his lurking place, cries out
" O Fools! the Road[1] is neither here nor there."

Ref. C. 396, L. 591, B. 584, S.P. 324, P. iii. 6, P. 65.—W. 376, N. 337,
V. 638.

XXVI.

This quatrain is taken from the following.

O 140.   آنان که زپیش رفته اند ای ساقی
در خاك غرور خفته اند ای ساقی
رو باده خور وحقیقت از من بشنو
باذمت هرآنچه گفته اند ای ساقی

Those, O Sākī, who have gone before us,

Have fallen asleep, O Sākī, in the dust (or *khwāb*
sleep) of self-esteem,

Go thou and drink wine, and hear the truth from me,

Whatever they have said, O Sākī, is but wind!

Ref.: O. 140, C. 453, L. 687, B. 678, S.P. 380, P. 260, B. ii. 525, T. 279,
P. v. 22.—W. 428, N. 384, V. 739.

C 236.   آنها که خلاصهٔ وجود انسانند
بر اوج فلك براق فكرت رانند
در معرفت ذات تو مانند فلك
سر گشته و سر نگون و سر گردانند

Those who are the cream of the existence of mankind,
Spur the Burāk of their thoughts up to the highest
heaven[2],

----

1   *i.e.*, the Mystic Road or Way of Salvation.
2   Burāk was the winged mule of Muhammad on which he is said to
    have journeyed from Jerusalem to heaven.

XXVII.

Myself when young did eagerly frequent
Doctor and Saint, and heard great argument
    About it and about: but evermore
Came out by the same door wherein I went.

XXVIII.

With them the seed of Wisdom did I sow,
And with mine own hand wrought to make it grow;
    And this was all the Harvest that I reap'd—
" I came like Water, and like Wind I go."

In the study of your being, like heaven itself
Their heads are turned, and overset, and spinning.

Ref.: C. 236, L. 326, B. 322, S.P. 120, T. 155, W. 147, N. 120, V. 328.

XXVII. & XXVIII.

These two quatrains must be considered together. They are inspired by the following.

O 121. یکچند بکودکـی باستـاد شدیم

یکچند باستادیٴ خود شاد شدیم

پایان سخن نگر که مارا چه رسید

چون آب در آمدیم وچون باد شدیم

For a while, when young, we frequented a teacher,
For a while we were contented with our proficiency;
Behold the end of the discourse:—what happened
       to us?
We came like water and we went like wind.

Ref.: O. 121, L. 544, B. 538, B. ii. 420, P. v. 99.—W. 353, V. 584.

C 281. بازی بودم پریدم از عالم راز

تابو که رسم ز پست علوی بفراز

اینجا چو نیافتم کس محرم راز

زان در که در آمدم برون رفتم باز

Being (once) a falcon, I flew from the World of mystery,
That from below I might soar to the heights above;

XXIX.

Into this Universe, and *Why* not knowing
Nor *Whence*, like Water willy-nilly flowing;
    And out of it, as Wind along the Waste,
I know not *Whither*, Willy-nilly blowing.

But, not finding there any intimate friend,
I came out by the same door wherein I went.[1]

Ref.: C. 281, L. 429, B. 425, S.P. 224, P. 30, B. ii, 295, T. 184—W. 264, N. 225, V. 467.

A quatrain that probably contributed to FitzGerald's verse is:

O 72. کس مشکل اسرار ازل را نکشاد
کس یك قدم از دایره بیرون ننهاد
چون بنگرم از مبتدی واز استاد
عجزمست بدست هرکه از مادر زاد

No one has solved the tangled secrets of eternity,
No one has set foot beyond the orbit (of human
  understanding),
Since, so far as I can see, from tyro to teacher,
Impotent are the hands of all men born of women.

Ref.: O. 72, C. 176, L. 357, B. 353, S.P. 175, B. ii. 211, P.v. 210— W. 190, N. 175, V. 356.

XXIX.

The inspiration for this quatrain is to be found in the following:

C 235. آورد باضطرابم آول بوجود
جز حیرتم از حیات چیزی نفزود
رفتیم باکراه و ندانیم چه بود
زین آمدن و رفتن و بودن مقصود

---

1 This is a very difficult quatrain to translate. The mystic soaring
  of the soul in search of enlightenment is compared to the flight of a
  falcon. In l. 3, *lit.*: "any partner of the secret."

XXX.

What, without asking, hither hurried *Whence ?*
And, without asking, *Whither* hurried hence!
   Oh, many a Cup of this forbidden Wine
Must drown the memory of that insolence!

He first brought me in confusion into existence,
What do I gain from my life save my amazement at it ?
We went away against our will, and we know not what was
The purpose of this coming, and going, and being.

Ref.: C. 235, L. 324, B. 320, S.P. 117, T. 153—W. 145, N. 117, V. 326.

O 20 ll 1 & 2.   چون آب بجویبار و چون باد بدشت

روزي دگر از نوبت عمرم بگذشت

Like water in a great river and like wind in the desert,
Another day passes out of the period of my existence.[1]

Ref.: O. 20, C. 23 and 55, L. 84, B. 80, S.P. 22, P. ii. 2, P. 162, B. ii. 24
and 88, T. 22 and 305, P. v. 140 and 186, W. 26, N. 22 and 42, V. 83.

XXX.

This quatrain owes its origin to two ruba'iyat in O.

O 21.   چون آمدلم بمن لبد روز لهست

وین رفتن بي‌مراد عزمیست درست

برخیز ومیان به بند ای‌ماقي چست

كاندوه جهان بمي فرو خواهم شست

Seeing that my coming was not in my power at the
Day of Creation,[2]
And that my undesired departure hence is a purpose
fixed (for me),
Get up and gird well thy loins, O nimble cup-bearer,
For I will wash down the misery of the world in wine.

Ref.: O. 21, C. 49, L. 94, B. 90, B. ii. 86, P. v. 123—W. 110, V. 94.

----

1 C. reads these two lines :—
    These two or three days of the period of my existence pass by
    They pass as passes the wind in the desert.
2 Compare FitzGerald's " First Morning of Creation " in q. 73.

4

XXXI.

Up from Earth's Centre through the Seventh Gate
I rose, and on the Throne of Saturn sate,
   And many a Knot unravel'd by the Road;
But not the Master-knot of Human Fate.

O 151. گـر آمـدنم بـن بدي لـامدمي

ورنيز شدن بـن بدي کي شدمي

به زان نبدي که اندرين عالم خاك

له آمـدمـي له شدمي نـه بدمي

Had I charge of the matter I would not have come,
And, likewise, could I control my going, how should I
    have gone?
There could have been nothing better than that in this
    world
I had neither come, nor gone, nor lived?

Ref.: O. 157, C. 494, L. 732, B. 720, P. 88. B. ii. 590 and 593, P. iv. 17,
P. v. 130—W. 490, E. C. 30, N. 450, V. 785.

XXXI.

This quatrain is translated from

C 314. از جّر حضيض خاك تا اوج زحل

کردم همه مشکلات گردون را حل

بيرون جستم ز بند هر مکر و حيل

هر مّد کشاده شد مگر بند اجل

From the Nadir of the earthly globe, up to the Zenith
    of Saturn
I solved all the problems of heaven;
I escaped from the bondage of all trickery and deceit,
All obstacles were removed save only the Bond of Fate.

Ref.: C. 314, L. 491, B. 487, B. ii. 338. T. 215—W. 303, V. 531.

4—2

XXXII.

There was the Door to which I found no Key;
There was the Veil through which I might not see:
    Some little talk awhile of ME and THEE
There was—and then no more of THEE and ME.

XXXII.

The main inspiration of this quatrain is found in

C 387.   اسرار ازل را نه تو دانی و نه من

وین حرف معمّا نه تو خوانی و نه من

هست از پس پرده گفتگوی من و تو

چون پرده برافتد نه تو مانی و نه من

Neither thou nor I know the secret of Eternity,
And neither thou nor I can de-cypher this riddle;
There is a talk behind the Curtain[1] of me and thee
But when the Curtain falls neither thou nor I are
there.

Ref.: C. 387, L. 581, B. 574, P. 33, B. ii. 421, T. 260—W. 389, V. 628.

———

We also see in the quatrain the influence of O. 29, and
C. 193.

O 29 ll 1 & 2.   در پرده اسرار کسی را ره نیست

زین تعبیه جان هیچکس آگه نیست

No one can pass behind the Curtain (that veils) the
secret,
The mind of no one is cognizant of what is there:[2]

Ref.: O. 29, C. 56, L. 61, B. 58, S.P. 43, P. 63, B. ii. 103, Pv. 188
—W. 47, N. 44, V. 60.

C 193 ll 1 & 2.   کس را پس پردۀ قصا راه نشد

وز سرّ قدر هیچ کس آگاه نشد

———

1   *i.e.*, the Curtain that Veils the Mysteries of God, a constantly recurring
image in Persian literature.
2   C. reads " of this juggling about of the soul."   E.B.C. suggests " of
this chess-opening."

XXXIII.*

Earth could not answer; nor the seas that mourn
In flowing Purple, of their Lord forlorn;
    Nor rolling Heaven, with all his Signs reveal'd
And hidden by the sleeve of Night and Morn.

No one can pass behind the Curtain of Fate
No one is master of the Secret of Destiny.

Ref.: C. 193, L. 345, B. 341, S.P. 177, B. ii. 212.—W. 192, N. 177, V. 346.

XXXIII.*

This is the quatrain (not No. 31 as stated by Mr. Aldis Wright in his Editorial Note) taken by Edward FitzGerald from the Mantik ut-tair of Ferid ud-dīn Attār. (*Vide* my former volume pp. xviii and xix.) The story which inspired it begins at distich No. 972, and is as follows :—

دیده ور مردی بدریا شد فرود
گفت ای دریا چرا داری کبود
جامهٔ مالم چرا پوشیدهٔ
نیست هیچ آتش چرا جوشیدهٔ
داد دریا آن لکو دل را جواب
کز فراق دوست دارم اضطراب
چو زنا مردی نیم من مرد او
جامه نیلی کرده ام از درد او

An observer of spiritual things approached the sea
And said "O sea, why are you blue?
"Why do you wear the robe of mourning?
"There is no fire, why do you boil?"
The sea made answer to that good-hearted one,
"I weep for my separation from the Friend,
"Since by reason of my impotence I am not worthy
of Him,
"I have made my robe blue on account of my sorrow
for Him."

XXXIV.

Then of the THEE IN ME who works behind
The Veil, I lifted up my hands to find
 A lamp amid the Darkness; and I heard,
As from Without—"THE ME WITHIN THEE BLIND!"

XXXV.

Then to the Lip of this poor earthen Urn
I lean'd, the Secret of my Life to learn;
 And Lip to Lip it murmur'd—"While you live,
"Drink!—for, once dead, you never shall return."

XXXIV.

That Edward FitzGerald was not following any particular ruba'iyat of the original MSS. is clearly indicated by the great variation observable in the forms that this quatrain successively assumed in the first, second and third editions. It suggests an exposition of the Sufi doctrine of the emanation of the mortal Creature from God the Creator, and his re-absorption into God. There is a quatrain in L. (No. 641) and in B. ii. (No. 457) which is akin to it, but FitzGerald was not acquainted with these texts. (It is No. 400 in W.) I have no doubt that FitzGerald's 34th quatrain was suggested to him by two intricate passages in the Mantik ut-tair, commencing respectively at distich 3090 and distich 3735. The first of these may be translated :

" The Creator of the World spoke thus to David from behind the Curtain of the Secret : ' For everything in the world, good or bad, visible or invisible, thou canst find a substitute, but for Me, thou canst find neither substitute nor equal. Since nothing can be substituted for Me, do not cease to abide in Me. I am thy Soul, destroy not thou thy Soul ; I am necessary to thee, O thou my servant. Seek not to exist apart from Me.' "

The second passage reads : " Since long ago, really, I am thee, and thou art Me ; we two are but One. Art thou Me, or am I thee ? is there any duality in the matter ? Either I am thee, or thou art Me, or thou, thou art thyself. Since thou art Me and I am thee for ever, our two bodies are One : Salutation ! "

___

XXXV.

This quatrain is translated from O. 100 :

O 100. لب برلب کوزه بردم از غایت آز
تا زو طلبم واسطهٔ عمـر دراز
لب برلب من نهاد ومی گفت براز
می خورکه بدین جهان نمی آیی باز

XXXVI.

I think the Vessel, that with fugitive
Articulation answer'd, once did live,
    And drink; and Ah! the passive Lip I kiss'd,
How many Kisses might it take—and give!

In great desire I pressed my lips to the lip of the jar,
To enquire from it how long life might be attained;
It joined its lip to mine and whispered,
" Drink wine! for to this world thou returnest not."

Ref.: O. 100, C. 283, L. 446, B. 442, P. 99, B. ii. 303, T. 185, P. v. 193
—W. 274, E. C. 25, V. 482.

C. 489 is a mystic and doctrinal quatrain containing the same injunction.

C 489 ll 3 & 4   مي خورکه هزار بار پيشت گفتم

باز آمدنت نيست چو رفتي رفتي

Drink wine! for I have told you a thousand times
There is no returning for you; when you are gone, you
are *gone!*

Ref.: C. 489, L. 723, B. 712, S. P. 385 B. ii. 526, P. iv. 67, P. v. 104—
W. 431, N. 389, V. 775.

XXXVI.

The inspiration for this quatrain occurs in O. 9.

O 9.   اين کوزه چو من عاشق زاري بودست

واندر طلب روي نگاري بودست

اين دسته که در گردن او مي بيني

دستيست که در گردن ياري بودست

This jug was once a plaintive lover, as I am,
And was in pursuit of one of comely face ;[1]
This handle that thou seest upon its neck
Is an arm that once lay around the neck of a friend.

Ref.: O. 9, C. 48 and 426, L. 81, B. 77, S. P. 28, P. 108, B. ii. 28,
P. v. 142—W. 32, N. 28, E. C. 5, V. 80.

----

1 C. reads "And was enslaved by the curly head of a sweetheart.'

XXXVII.

For I remember stopping by the way
To watch a Potter thumping his wet Clay;
    And with its all-obliterated Tongue
It murmur'd—"Gently, Brother, gently, pray!"

XXXVIII.*

And has not such a Story from of Old
Down Man's successive generations roll'd
    Of such a clod of saturated Earth
Cast by the maker into Human mould?

XXXVII.

The original of this quatrain is O. 89.

O 89.   دی کوزہگـری بدیدم اندر بازار
بر تازہ گلی لکد همی زد بسیار
وآن گل بزبان حال با او می گفت
من همچو تو بودہ ام مرا نیکو دار

I saw a potter in the bazaar yesterday,
He was violently pounding some fresh clay,
And that clay said to him in mystic language,
" I was once like thee—so treat me well."

Ref.: O. 89, C. 261, L. 411, B. 407, S.P. 210, P. 100, B. ii. 274, P. iv. 71,
P.v. 198.—W. 252, N. 211, V. 434.

XXXVIII.*

This quatrain, which is in the nature of a reflection upon
the three preceeding ones, conveys an idea which is constantly
recurrent in the ruba'iyat. Edward FitzGerald himself records,
in a note, that, in composing this quatrain, he had in mind a
very beautiful story in the Mantik ut-tair of the water of a
certain well which, ordinarily sweet, became bitter when
drawn in a vessel made from clay which once had been a man.
For its inclusion in this poem FitzGerald had the support of
two (among many) quatrains from C.

C 475.   در کارگه کوزہگری کردم رای
در مائہ چرخ دیدم استاد بپای
میکرد سبو و کوزہرا دستہ و سر
ازکلّهٔ پادشاہ و از پای گدای

XXXIX.*

And not a drop that from our Cups we throw
For Earth to Drink of, but may steal below
    To quench the fire of Anguish in some Eye
There hidden—far beneath and long ago.

I pondered over the workshop of a potter;
In the shadow of the wheel I saw that the master, with
     his feet,
Made handles and covers for goblets and jars,
Out of the skulls of kings and the feet of beggars.

Ref.: C. 475, L. 698, B. 689, S.P. 426, P. 103, B.ii. 576—W. 466, N. 431,
V. 750.

C 488.   بر کوزہگران دھر کردم گذری

از خاك همی شود هر دم هنری

من دیدم اگر ندید هر بی بصری

خاك پدرم بر كف هر کوزہگری

I made my way into the (abode of the) potters of the
     age,
Every moment shewed some new skill with clay;
I saw, though men devoid of vision saw it not,
My ancestors' dust on the hands of every potter.

Ref.: C. 488, L. 721, B. 710, P. 101, B.ii. 543—W. 493, V. 773.

XXXIX.*

This quatrain is taken from ll. 1 and 2 of O. 81.

O 81 ll 1 & 2.   هر جرعه که ماقیش بخاك افشالد

در دیدهٔ گـرم آتش غم بشالد

Every draught that the Cup-bearer scatters upon the earth
Quenches the fire of anguish in some burning eye.

Ref.: O. 81, C. 180, L. 367, B. 363, S. P. 188, P. 231, B. ii. 241, P. v. 187,
W. 203, N. 188, V. 366.

XL.*

As then the Tulip for her morning sup
Of Heav'nly Vintage from the soil looks up,
    Do you devoutly do the like, till Heav'n
To Earth invert you—like an empty Cup.

XLI.*

Perplext no more with Human or Divine,
To-morrow's tangle to the winds resign,
    And lose your fingers in the tresses of
The Cypress-slender Minister of Wine.

XL.*

The original of this quatrain is

C 37. چون لاله بنوروز قدح گیر بدست

با ماه رخی اگر ترا فرصت هست

می نوش بخرمی که این چرخ کهن

ناگاه تراچو خاك گرداند پست

Like a tulip in the spring uplift your cup ;
If you get a (happy) opportunity with a moon-faced one,
Drink wine with cheerfulness, for this worn-out sky
Will suddenly invert you to the level of the earth.

Ref.: C. 37, L. 136, B. 133, S. P. 39, B. ii. 84, T. 40 and 311—W. 44, N. 40, V. 135.

XLI.*

The sentiment of this quatrain is very recurrent. I think that FitzGerald's first inspiration comes from :

O 73. کمکن طمع ازجهان ومی زی خرسند

وز نیك وبد زمانه بگسل پیوند

می برکف و زلف دلبری گیر که زود

هم بگذرد ونماند این روزی چند

Set limits to thy desire for worldly things and live content,
Sever the bonds of thy dependence upon the good and bad
      of life,
Take wine in hand and (play with) the curls of a loved
      one; for quickly
All passeth away—and these few days will not remain.

Ref.: O. 73, C. 179, L. 256, B. 253, S. P. 176—W. 191, N. 176, V. 262.

XLII.

And if the Wine you drink, the Lip you press,
End in what All begins and ends in—Yes;
    Think then you are TO-DAY what YESTERDAY
You were—TO-MORROW you shall not be less.

Ll. 3 and 4 of O. 118 suggest the quatrain also.

O 118 ll 3 & 4   دست از امل دراز خود باز کشیم

در زلف دراز ودامن چنگ زلیم

Let us cease to strive after our long delaying hope[1]
And play with long ringlets and the handle of the lute.

Ref.: O. 118, L. 571, B. 564, S. P. 293, B. ii. 391—W. 332, N. 294, V. 611.

Ll. 1 and 2 of O. 131 is also in point:

O 131 ll 1 & 2   از درس علوم جمله بگریزی به

واندر سر زلف دلبر آویزی به

Flee from the study of all sciences—'tis better thus,
And twine thy fingers in the curly locks of a loved
one—'tis better thus.

Ref.: O. 131, C. 443, L. 670, B. 662, S.P. 356, P. 296, B.ii. 480, T. 276, P.v. 158—W. 426, N. 359, V. 719.

FitzGerald was probably " reminded of " these by Nicolas whose quatrains 48, 155, and 359 (C. 443) convey the same idea.

XLII.

The inspiration for this quatrain is contained in the following :

O 102.   خیّام اگر زباده مستی خوش باش

با لاله رخی اگر نشستی خوش باش

چون آخر کار نیست خواهی بودن

انگارکه نیستی چو هستی خوش باش

----

1   *i.e.*, " Let us cease striving to earn salvation."

XLIII.

So when that Angel of the darker Drink
At last shall find you by the river-brink,
    And, offering his Cup, invite your Soul
Forth to your Lips to quaff—you shall not shrink.

Khayyām, if thou art drunk with wine,[1] be happy,
If thou reposest with one tulip-cheeked, be happy,
Since the end of all things is that thou wilt be naught;
Whilst thou art, imagine that thou art not—be happy!

Ref.: O. 102, C. 291, L. 454, B. 450, S.P. 241, P. 202, B.ii. 322, T. 192
and 296, P.iv. 26, P.v. 5—W. 282, N. 242, V. 493.

C 412.   روزیکه ز تو گذشته است یاد مکن

فردا که نیامدست بیداد مکن

وز آمده و گذشته خود یاد مکن

حالی می نوش و عمر بر باد مکن

Remember not the day that has passed away from thee,
Be not hard upon the morrow that has not come,
Think not about thine own coming or departure,
Drink wine *now*, and fling not thy life to the winds.

Ref.: C. 412, L. 619, B. 611, P. 116, B. ii. 444, P. v. 121—V. 666.

<hr>

XLIII.

This quatrain owes its origin to C. 256.[2]

C 256.   در دایرهٔ سپهر ناپیدا غور

جامیست که جمله‌را چشانند بدور

چون نوبت تو رسد تو هم آه مکن

می نوش بخوشدلی که دورست بخور

In the circle of the firmament, whose depths are
    invisible,
There is a cup which, in due time, they will cause all
    to drink;

<hr>

1 C. reads "with love."
2 FitzGerald records in his note to this quatrain that had it not been
   for the advice of Prof. Cowell, this and the two following quatrains
   would have been withdrawn after the Second Edition. It is impossible to conceive why, for they are singularly fine and exception-
   ally " authorized."

XLIV.

Why, if the Soul can fling the Dust aside,
And naked on the Air of Heaven ride,
    Were't not a Shame—were't not a Shame for him
In this clay carcase crippled to abide?

XLV.

'Tis but a Tent where takes his one day's rest
A Sultán to the realm of Death addrest;
    The Sultán rises, and the dark Ferrásh
Strikes, and prepares it for another Guest.

When thy turn comes, do not utter lamentations,
Drink wine gaily for it has come to be thy turn.

Ref. : C. 256, L. 408, B. 404, B. ii. 273—W. 254, V. 431.

XLIV.

This quatrain is translated from O. 145.

O 145. اى دل زغبار جسم اگر پاك شوى

تو روح مجردى بر افلاك شوى

عرشست نشيمن تو شرمت بادا

كائى ومقيم خطهٔ خاك شوى

Oh Soul! if thou canst purify thyself from the dust of
the body,
Thou, naked spirit, canst soar in the heavens,
The Empyrean is thy sphere—let it be thy shame,
That thou comest and art a dweller within the confines
of earth.[1]

Ref. : O. 145, C. 447, L. 707, B. 697, S. P. 389, P. 111, B. ii. 523—
W. 436, N. 394, E. C. 7, V. 759.

XLV.

This quatrain is translated from C. 110.

C 110. خيام تنت بخيمهٔ ماند راست

جان سلطان است و منزلش دار فناست

فراش اجل ز بهر ديگر منزل

اين خيمه بيفكند چو سلطان بر خاست

---

1 FitzGerald's rendering in the 1st edition (Introduction), "in this clay
suburb" is a more literal rendering.

XLVI.*

And fear not lest Existence closing your
Account, and mine, should know the like no more;
    The Eternal Sáki from that Bowl has pour'd
Millions of Bubbles like us, and will pour.

XLVII.*

When You and I behind the Veil are past,
Oh, but the long, long while the World shall last,
    Which of our Coming and Departure heeds
As the Sea's self should heed a pebble-cast.

Khayyām! thy body surely resembles a tent;
The soul is a Sultān and the halting place is the perish-
able world,
The ferrash of fate, preparing for the next halting place,
Will overthrow this tent when the Sultān has arisen.[1]

Ref.: C. 110, L. 100, B. 96, S.P. 80, B.ii. 95, T. 86, P.v. 172—W. 82,
N. 80, V. 100.

XLVI.*

FitzGerald was indebted for this quatrain to N. 137. The
original ruba'i is not in O. or C.

N 137.   خیام اگر چه خرگهٔ چرخ کبود
زد خیمه و در بست در گفت و شنود
چون شکل حباب باده درجام وجود
ساقی ازل هزار خیام نمود

Khayyām! although the pavilion of heaven
Has spread its tent and closed the door upon all
discussion,
In the goblet of existence, like bubbles of wine
The Eternal Sākī brings to light a thousand Khayyāms.

Ref.: N. 137,[2] W. 161, V. 397.

XLVII.*

In this quatrain FitzGerald is "reminded of" O. 26
and 51 by N. 123.

O 26 ll 1 & 2.   دریاب که از روح جدا خواهی رفت
در پردهٔ اسرار خدا خواهی رفت

---

1 *i.e.*, The ferrash of fate, preparing for the next halting-place, destroys
   this tent (body) when the Sultān (soul) arises.
2 I do not know the origin of N.'s text, but I have never seen this
   quatrain in any other MS. The same remark applies to N. 123,
   cited under No. 47.

XLVIII.

A Moment's Halt—a momentary taste
Of BEING from the Well amidst the waste—
    And Lo!—the phantom Caravan has reach'd
The NOTHING it set out from—Oh, make haste!

Know this—that from thy soul thou shalt be separated,
Thou shalt pass behind the Curtain of the Secrets of God.

Ref. : O. 26, C. 83, L. 192, B. 189, S. P. 85, B. ii. 110, T. 64, P. v. 34—
W. 87, N. 85, V. 188.

O 51 ll 1 & 2.   از آمدنم نبود گردونرا سود

وز رفتن من جمال وجاهش نفزود

My coming was of no profit to the heavenly sphere,[1]
And by my departure nothing will be added to its beauty
and dignity.

Ref. : O. 51, C. 129, L. 232, B. 229, S. P. 157, P. 55, B. ii. 158, T. 104—
W. 176, N. 157. E. C. 17, V. 239.

N 123.   ای بس که لباشیم و جهان خواهد بود

بی نام ز ما و بی نشان خواهد بود

زین پیش نبودیم و نبد هیچ خلل

زین پس چو لباشیم و همان خواهد بود

Oh! how long we shall be no more, and the world will
continue to exist,
It will continue to exist without fame or sign of us,
Long ago we existed not, and (the world) was none the
worse for it,
Afterwards, when we have ceased to exist, it will be all
the same.

Ref. : N. 123, W. 150, V. 395.

XLVIII.

We must consider here the form in which this quatrain
first made its appearance in the edition of 1859:

---

1 C. reads " From my creation the Age derived no advantage."

XLIX.*

Would you that spangle of Existence spend
About THE SECRET—quick about it, Friend !
    A Hair perhaps divides the False and True—
And upon what, prithee, may life depend ?

L.*

A Hair perhaps divides the False and True ;
Yes ; and a single Alif were the clue—
    Could you but find it—to the Treasure-house,
And peradventure to THE MASTER too ;

One Moment in Annihilation's Waste,
One Moment, of the Well of Life to taste—
    The stars are setting, and the Caravan
Starts for the Dawn of Nothing—Oh, make haste!

The inspiration for this richly varied quatrain comes from
O. 60.

O 60. این قافله' عمر عجب می گذرد

دریاب دمی که با طرب می گذرد

ساقی غم فردای حریفان چه خوری

دردہ قدح باده که شب میگذرد

This caravan of life passes by mysteriously;
Mayest thou seize the moment that passes happily!
Cup-bearer, why grieve about the to-morrow of thy
    patrons ? [1]
Give us a cup of wine, for the night wanes.

Ref.: O. 60, C. 135, L. 245, B. 242, P. 223, S.P. 106, B.ii. 146, T. 139—
W. 136, N. 106, V. 251.

    Ll. 3 and 4 of C. 368 may also be quoted :

C 368 ll 3 & 4. محنت زدہ' سرشته الدر گل غم

یکچند جهان بخورد و داشت قدم

(Man is) a toil-stricken being, fashioned in the clay of
    affliction,
He tasted of Earth for a time and passed away.

Ref.: C. 368, L. 566, B. 559, S. P. 301, B. ii. 404, T. 242—W. 338,
N. 302, V. 606.

XLIX* & L.*

This pair of quatrains must also be considered together.

---

1 *Harifan ;* literally, " companions," " fellow-workers."

The idea contained in them is, I think, collected from the
following :

C 482.

چون واقفى اى پسر ز هر اسرارى

چندين چه برى به بيهده تيمارى

چون مى نرود باختيارت كارى

خوش باش درين نفس كه هستى بارى

Oh Boy! since thou art learned in all secrets,
Why grieve so much after vain cares?
If things will not shape themselves according to thy desire,
At any rate be happy in this moment of thy existence.

Ref.: C. 482, L. 714, B. 703, S. P. 414, B. ii. 560—W. 458, N. 419, V. 766.

C 19.

از منزل كفر تا بدين يكنفس اميست

وز عالم شك تا بيقين يكنفس است

اين يكنفس عزيزرا خوش ميدار

كز حاصل عمر ما همين يكنفس است

From the state of infidelity to that of faith is but a breath,
And from a state of doubt to that of certainty is but a
        breath,
Hold thou dear this one precious moment,
For of the outcome of our being there is but a moment.

Ref.: C. 19, L. 131, B. 127, S. P. 20, B. ii. 22, T. 20—W. 24, N. 20,
V. 130.

O 28.

دل گفت مرا علم لدنّي هوس است

تعليمم كن اگر ترا دمست رس است

گفتم كه الف گفت دگر هيچ مگو

درخانه اگر كس است يك حرف بس است

LI.*

Whose secret Presence, through Creation's veins
Running Quicksilver-like eludes your pains;
    Taking all shapes from Máh to Máhí; and
They change and perish all—but He remains;

My Heart said to me: "I have a longing for inspired
  knowledge,
"Teach me if thou art able,"
I said the Alif. My Heart said: "Say no more.
"If One is in the house, one letter is enough."[1]
Ref.: O. 28—W. 109.

LI.*

In this quatrain FitzGerald has made a masterly con-
version of C. 72.

C 72. آن ماه که قابل صور هامست بذاتست

گاها حیوان میشود و گاه نباتست

تا ظن نبری که نیست گردد هیهات

موصوف بذاتست اگر لیست صفاتست

That Moon which is by nature skilled in metamorphosis
Is sometimes animal and sometimes vegetable,
Do not imagine that it will become non-existent—away
  with thought!
It is always possessed of its essence though its qualities
  cease to be.[2]
Ref.: C. 72, L. 179, B. 176, S.P. 73, B.ii. 31, T. 51—W. 75, N. 73, V. 175.

C. 40 may also be cited.

C 40. می بر کف من نه که دلم در تابست

ولین عمر گریز پای چون سیمابست

بر خیز که بیداری دولت خوابست

دریاب که آتش جوانی آب آمست

---

1 *i.e.*, The One God. Compare Háfiz (Ode 416), "He who knows the
  One, knows all."
2 Prof. Cowell's translation. V. appends a note, "Apparently the
  Essence of Life, the *Ding an Sich* of Kant, and the *Wille* of
  Schopenhauer, the Platonic Idea, the abiding type of the
  perishable individuality; possibly, however, the Vedantic 'self'
  is meant." For the word *mah* = moon at the commencement of
  the quatrain, some of the texts read *badeh* = wine.

6

LII.*

A moment guess'd—then back behind the Fold
Immerst of Darkness round the Drama roll'd
    Which, for the Pastime of Eternity,
He doth Himself contrive, enact, behold.

LIII.*

But if in vain, down on the stubborn floor
Of Earth, and up to Heav'n's unopening Door,
    You gaze TO-DAY, while You and You—how then
TO-MORROW, when You shall be You no more?

Place wine in my hand for my heart is aglow,
And this fleet-footed existence is like quicksilver.
Arise! for the wakefulness of good fortune turns to slumber;
Know thou that the fire of youth is (fugitive) like water.

Ref.: C. 40, L. 63, B. 60. S. P. 54, T. 45—W. 57, N. 54, V. 62.

"From Mah to Mahi"—*i.e.*, from Moon to Fish is a common Oriental metaphor for universality. See FitzGerald's note on this subject, and the Terminal Essay to my former volume p. 309.

LII.*

This quatrain is translated from C. 479.

C 479. که گشته نهان رو بکسی ننمائي
که در صور کون و مکان پیدائي
این جلوه گري بخویشتن ننمائي
خود عین عیان خودي و هم بینائي

Hidden sometimes thou shewest thy face to none,
Sometimes thou appearest in the forms of created beings,
Thou exhibitest this spectacle to thyself.
Thou art thyself both the real thing seen and the spectator.

Ref.: C. 479, L. 705, B. 695, S. P. 437—W. 475, N. 443, V. 757.

LIII.*

The original of this quatrain is C. 24.

C 24. دل سرّ حیات اگر کما هي دانست
در موت هم اسرار الهي دانست
امروز که با خودي ندانستي هیچ
فردا که ز خود روي چه خواهي دانست

LIV.

Waste not your Hour, nor in the vain pursuit
Of this and That endeavour and dispute;
  Better be jocund with the fruitful Grape
Than sadden after none, or Bitter Fruit.

If the heart understood the secret of existence as it *is*,
In death it would know all the secrets of God:
If to-day thou knowest nothing, being *with* thyself,
What wilt thou know to-morrow when thou abandonest
 thyself?

Ref.: C. 24, L. 78, B. 74, S. P. 49, P. 85, B. ii. 106, T. 25—W. 52,
N. 49, V. 77.

LIV.

The inspiration for this quatrain comes from the
following :

O 50. آنان كه امير عقل وتمييز شدند
در حسرت هست ونيست ناچيز شدند
رو بيخبري وآب انگور گزين
كـان بيخبران بغوره ميويز شدند

Those who are the slaves of intellect and hair-splitting,[1]
Have perished in bickerings about existence and non-
 existence ;
Go, thou dunce ! and choose (rather) grape juice,
For the ignorant from (eating) dry raisins, have become
 (like) unripe grapes (themselves).[2]

Ref.: O. 50, L. 262, T. 102, P.v. 164—W. 216, V. 267.

O 107. تا كي ز ابد حديث وتا كي ز ازل
هنگام طرب شرابـرا نيست بدل
بگذشت ز اندازه من علم وعمل
هر مشكلرا شراب گـرداند حل

---

1 Literally, " discernment."
2 The obscurity of the meaning here baffles satisfactory translation.
  Prof. Cowell says: I would rather take it as a sarcasm, " Those
  fools with their unripe grapes become (in their own eyes) pure
  wine " (ميويز).

LV.

You know, my friends, with what a brave Carouse
I made a Second Marriage in my house;
    Divorced old barren Reason from my Bed,
And took the Daughter of the Vine to Spouse.

LVI.

For " Is " and " Is-not " though with Rule and Line
And " Up-and-down " by Logic I define,
    Of all that one should care to fathom, I
Was never deep in anything but—Wine.

How long this talk about the eternity to come, and the
  eternity past ?[1]
Now is the time of joy, there is no substitute for wine!
Both theory and practice have passed beyond my ken,
(But) Wine unties the knot of every difficulty.

Ref.: O. 107, C. 312, L. 489, B. 485, B.ii. 341, T. 213, P.v. 207—W. 304,
V. 259.

LV.

This quatrain is translated from C. 175.

C 175.   من باده بجام یکمنی خواهم کرد

خودرا بدو رطل می غنی خواهم کرد

اول سه طلاق عقل و دین خواهم گفت

پس دختر رزرا بزنی خواهم کرد

I will fill a one-maund goblet with wine,
I will enrich myself with two half-maunds of wine:
First I will thrice pronounce the divorce from learning
  and faith,[2]
And then I will take the daughter of the vine[3] to spouse.

Ref.: C. 175, L. 267, B. 263, P. 288, P.v. 209—V. 271.

LVI.

This quatrain is translated from O. 120:

O 120.   مـن ظاهـر لیستی وهستی دالم

مـن باطن هـر فراز ویستی دالم

با این همه از دالش خود شرمم باد

گـر مـرتبـه ورای مستی دالم

---

1 *Azal* in Persian dogma is eternity without beginning, *i.e.,* "*from* all
   time," as opposed to *abad,* eternity without end, *i.e.,* "*to* all
   eternity."

2 In the East a man may divorce his wife twice and take her back
   again, but the third time it is irrevocable—unless (curiously
   enough) she has been married to someone else in the meantime.

3 *i.e.,* Wine, a recurrent Persian metaphor. Comp.: Arabic "*bint-ul-
   kerm.*"

LVII.*

Ah, but my Computations, People say,
Reduced the Year to better reckoning ?—Nay,
  'Twas only striking from the Calendar
Unborn To-morrow and dead Yesterday.

I know the outwardness of existence and non-existence,[1]
I know the inwardness of all that is high and low;
Nevertheless let me be ashamed of[2] my own knowledge
If I recognise any degree higher than drunkenness.

Ref.: O. 120, L. 523, B. 518, S. P. 299, P. 265, B. ii. 409, P. v. 38—
W. 336, N. 300, V. 563.

LVII.*

This quatrain owes its inspiration to the following :

C 381.
دشمن بغلط گفت که من فلسفیم
ایزد داند که آنچه او گفت نیم
لیکن چو درین غم آشیان آمده ام
اخر کم از آن که من ندالم که کیم

My enemies erroneously have called me a philosopher,[3]
God knows I am not what they have called me ;
But, as I have come into this nesting place of sorrow,
In the end I am in a still worse plight, for I know not
who I am.

Ref.: C. 381, L. 580, B. 573, B.ii. 383, T. 259—W. 350, V. 619.

O 20 ll 3 & 4.
هرگز غم دو روز مرا یاد نکشت
روزی که نیامدست و روز که گذشت

Never has grief lingered in my mind concerning two
days,[4]

---

1 *Zahir* = exoteric, as opposed to *batin* = esoteric, in line 2.
2 C. reads " I am weary."
3 The opening lines of FitzGerald's quatrain refer to Omar's reforma-
tion of the calendar, and institution of the Jalāli era, which
Gibbon describes as "a computation of time which surpassed
the Julian, and approached the accuracy of the Gregorian style."
(" Decline and Fall of the Roman Empire," Gibbing's edition,
1890, vol. iv., p. 180.)
4 C. reads " So long as I live, I will not grieve for two days."

LXIII.

And lately, by the Tavern Door agape,
Came shining through the Dusk an Angel Shape
 Bearing a vessel on his Shoulder ; and
He bid me taste of it ; and 'twas—the Grape !

LIX.

The Grape that can with Logic absolute
The Two-and-Seventy jarring Sects confute ;
 The sovereign Alchemist that in a trice
Life's leaden metal into Gold transmute ;

The day that has not yet come, and the day that is past.

Ref.: O. 20, C. 23 and 55, L. 84, S.P. 22, B. 80, P. 162, B.ii. 24 and 88, P.ii. 2, T. 22 and 305, P.v. 140 and 186—W. 26, N. 22 and 42, V. 83.

LVIII.

This quatrain is a refined version of C. 297.

C 297. سر مست بميخانه گذر کردم دوش
پيری ديدم مست و مبوئي بر دوش
گفتم ز خدا شرم نداری ای پير
گفتا کرم از خداست رو باده بنوش

Yesterday, whilst drunk, I was passing a tavern,
I saw a drunken old man bearing a vessel on his shoulder.
I said, "Old man, does not God make thee ashamed?"
He replied, "God is merciful, go, drink wine!"

Ref. : C. 297, L. 462, B. 458, S. P. 243, P. 278, T, 197—W. 284, N. 244 V. 501.

LIX.

This quatrain is translated from O. 77.

O 77. می خور که زتو کثرت علت ببرد
والديشه هفتاد و دو ملت ببرد
پرهيز مکن زکيميائي که ازو
يك جرعه خوري هزار علت ببرد

Drink wine, that will banish thine abundant woes.
And will banish thought of the Seventy-two Sects;

LX.

The mighty Mahmúd, Allah-breathing Lord,
That all the misbelieving and black Horde
    Of Fears and Sorrows that infest the Soul
Scatters before him with his whirlwind Sword.

LXI.*

Why, be this Juice the growth of God, who dare
Blaspheme the twisted tendril as a Snare?
    A Blessing, we should use it, should we not?
And if a Curse—Why, then, Who set it there?

Avoid not the Alchemist,[1] from whom
Thou takest one draught, and he banishes a thousand
calamities.

Ref.: O. 77, C. 165, L. 305, B. 301, S.P. 179, P. 283, T. 112, P. v. 152.—
W. 194, V. 308.

_____

LX.

This reference to Mahmoud the Ghasnavide, who made war
upon the black infidels of Hindostan, comes from an apologue
in the Mantik ut-tair of Ferid ud-dīn Attār, (beginning at
distich 3117). The last two lines come from O. 81, ll.
3 and 4.

O 81 ll 3 & 4. سبحـان الله تو باده مى پندارى

آبى كه زصد درد دلت برهـاند

Praise be to God! thou realizest that wine
Is a juice that frees thy heart from a hundred pains.

Ref.: O. 81, C. 180, L. 367, B. 363, S.P. 188, P. 231, B. ii. 241, P. v.
187.—W. 203, N. 188, V. 366.

_____

LXI.*

The inspiration for this quatrain is contained in O. 75.

O 75. مى مى‌خورم وهركه چو من اهل بود

مى خوردن من بنزد او مهل بود

مى خوردن من حق بازل مى‌دانست

گر مى نخورم علم خدا جهل بود

I drink wine, and everyone drinks who, like me, is
worthy of it ;
My wine-drinking is but a small thing to Him ;

_____

1   *i.e.*, Wine.

LXII.*

I must abjure the Balm of Life, I must,
Scared by some After-reckoning ta'en on trust,
    Or lured with Hope of some Diviner Drink,
To fill the Cup—when crumbled into Dust!

God knew on the Day of Creation, that I should drink
wine;
If I do not drink wine God's knowledge would be
ignorance.

Ref.: O. 75, C. 202, L. 356, B. 352, S. P. 182, P. 324, B. ii. 234, T. 129,
Pv. 181—W. 197, N. 182, V. 355.

LXII.*

This quatrain is taken from the following:

C 505. گویند مخور می که بلاکش باشی
در روز مکافات بر آتش باشی
این هست ولی هر دوجهان می ارزد
آن یکدمه کز شراب سر خوش باشی

They say, " Do not drink wine for thou wilt suffer for it,
On the Day of Rewards thou wilt be cast into the fire,
That is so; but what is worth both the worlds
Is the moment when thou art elated with wine.

Ref.: C. 505, L. 748, B. 734, P. 250, B.ii. 587—V. 800.

O 143 ll 3 & 4. اینجا بمی وجام بهشتی می ساز
کانجا که بهشتست رسی یا نرسی

Make thyself a heaven here with wine and cup,
For at that place where heaven is, thou mayst arrive,
or mayst not.

Ref.: O. 143, C. 495, L. 733, B. 721, S.P. 379, P. 209, B.ii. 529, P.v. 129
—W. 427, N. 383, V. 786.

LXIII.

Oh threats of Hell and Hopes of Paradise!
One thing at least is certain—*This* Life flies;
  One thing is certain and the rest is Lies;
The Flower that once has blown for ever dies.

LXIV.*

Strange, is it not? that of the myriads who
Before us pass'd the door of Darkness through,
  Not one returns to tell us of the Road,
Which to discover we must travel too.

LXIII.

The inspiration for this quatrain comes from O. 35 of
which ll. 1 and 2 are quoted as parallel to quatrain No. 24
ante.

O 35 ll 3 & 4. زنهار بکس مگو تو این راز نهفت

هــر لاله° که پژمــرد نخواهد بشکفت

Take care that thou tellest not this hidden secret to
anyone :

The tulips that are withered will never bloom again.

Ref.: O. 35, C. 80, L. 188, B. 185, P. 284, T. 60—W. 107, V. 184.

LXIV.*

This is a constantly recurring image in the ruba'iyat.
The following may be cited :

C 36. بسیار بگشتیم بگرد در و دشت

الدرهمه آفاق بگشتیم بگشت

از کس نشیدیم که آمد زان راه

راهی که برفت راه رو باز نگشت

I have travelled far in a wandering by valley and desert,
It came to pass I wandered in all quarters of the world,
I have not heard from anyone who came from that road,
The road he has travelled, no traveller travels again.

Ref.: C. 36, L. 57, B. 54, T. 39—W. 129, V. 56.

C 270. از جمله° رفتگان این راه دراز

باز آمده° کو که بما گوید راز

زنهار درین سراچه از روی مجاز

چیزی نگذاری که نیائی باز

7

LXV.*

The Revelations of Devout and Learn'd
Who rose before us, and as Prophets burn'd,
    Are all but Stories, which, awoke from Sleep,
They told their comrades, and to Sleep return'd.

LXVI.*

I sent my Soul through the Invisible,
Some letter of that After-life to spell:
    And by and by my Soul return'd to me,
And answer'd, "I myself am Heav'n and Hell:"

Of all the travellers upon this long road,
Where is he that has returned, that he may tell us the
 secret ?
Take heed that in this mansion (by way of metaphor)
Thou leavest nothing, for thou wilt not come back.

Ref. : C. 270, L. 424, B. 420, S. P. 216, P. 121, B. ii. 286, P. v. 9
—W. 258, N. 217, V. 462.

C. 211 and 277 contain the same image.

LXV.*

This quatrain is translated from C. 127.

C 127. آنان که محیط فضل و آداب شدند

از جمع کمال شمع اصحاب شدند

ره زین‌شب تاریک نبردند برون

گفتند فسانه‌ٔ و در خواب شدند

Those who have become oceans of excellence and culti-
 vation,
And from the collection of their perfections have become
 lights of their fellows,
Have not made a road out of this dark night,
They have told a fable and have gone to sleep.

Ref. : C. 127, L. 261, B. 258, P. 86, T. 101—W. 209, N. 464, V. 266.

LXVI.*

This quatrain is inspired by O. 15.

O 15. برتر ز سپهر خاطرم روز نخست

لوح وقلم وبهشت و دوزخ می جست

پس گفت مرا معلّم از رای درست

لوح وقلم وبهشت و دوزخ با تُست

LXVII.*

Heav'n but the Vision of fulfill'd Desire,
And Hell the Shadow from a Soul on fire,
    Cast on the Darkness into which Ourselves,
So late emerged from, shall so soon expire.

Already on the Day of Creation, beyond the heavens,.
  my soul
Searched for the Tablet and Pen, and for heaven and hell;
At last the Teacher said to me with His enlightened
  judgment,
"Tablet and Pen, and heaven and hell, are within
  thyself."[1]

Ref.: O 15, L. 59, B. 56, P. 114, B. ii. 69, P. v. 79.—W. 114, V. 58.

LXVII.*

The inspiration for this verse comes from O. 33.

O 33. گردون کمری از تن فرسودهٔ ماست

جیهون اثری ز اشك پالودهٔ ماست

دوزخ شرری ز رنج بیهودهٔ ماست

فردوس دمي ز وقت آسوده° ماست

The heavenly vault is a girdle (cast) from my weary body.
Jihun[2] is a water-course worn by my filtered tears,
Hell is a spark from my useless worries,
Paradise is a moment of time when I am tranquil.

Ref.: O. 33, C. 90, L. 199, B. 196, S.P. 90, P. 148, T. 70, P.v. 183—
W. 92, N. 90, V. 195.

FitzGerald's verse was evidently also influenced by distich
1866 of the Mantik ut-tair.

طاعت روحانیان بهر تست

خلد و دوزخ عكس لطف و قهر تست

---

1 The *Lauh u Kalam* are the Tablet and Pen whereon and wherewith
  the Divine decrees of what should be from all time were written.
  Compare Qur'ān, ch. lxviii, 1. "By the Pen and what they write,
  O Muhammad! thou art not distracted."
2 *i.e.*, the river Oxus.

LXVIII.

We are no other than a moving row
Of Magic Shadow-shapes that come and go
    Round with the Sun-illumined Lantern held
In Midnight by the Master of the Show;

LXIX.

But helpless Pieces of the Game He plays
Upon this Chequer-board of Nights and Days;
    Hither and thither moves, and checks, and slays,
And one by one back .in the Closet lays.

Heaven and hell are reflections, the one of thy goodness,
and the other of thy wrath.

LXVIII.

This quatrain is translated from O. 108.

O 108. این چرخ فلك که ما درو حیرانیم

فانوس خیال ازو مثالی دانیم

خورشید چراغ دان وعالم فانوس

ما چون صوریم کاندرو گردانیم

This vault of heaven beneath which we stand bewildered,
We know to be a sort of magic-lantern : [1]
Know thou that the sun is the flame and the universe
is the lamp,
We are like figures that revolve in it.

Ref.: O. 108, C. 332, L. 505, B. 501, S.P. 266, P. 40, B.ii. 356, P.iv. 34
—W. 310, N. 267, E.C. 28, de T. 10, V. 545.

LXIX.

This quatrain is translated from O. 94.

O 94. از روي حقیقتی له از روي مجاز

ما لعبتگانیم وفلك لعبت باز

بازیچه همي کنیم بر لطع وجود

رفتیم بصندوق عدم یك یك باز

---

[1] The editor of the *Calcutta Review* appends the following note at the foot of Prof. Cowell's article (E.C.) " These lanthorns are very common in Calcutta. They are made of a tall cylinder with figures of men and animals cut out of paper and pasted on it. The cylinder, which is very light, is suspended on an axis, round which it easily turns. A hole is cut near the bottom, and the part cut out is fixed at an angle to the cylinder so as to form a vane. When a small lamp or candle is placed inside, a current of air is produced which keeps the cylinder slowly revolving."

LXX.

The Ball no question makes of Ayes and Noes
But Here or There as strikes the Player goes ;
    And He that toss'd you down into the Field,
He knows about it all—HE knows—HE knows!

LXXI.

The Moving Finger writes; and, having writ,
Moves on : nor all your Piety nor Wit
    Shall lure it back to cancel half a Line,
Nor all your Tears wash out a Word of it.

To speak plain language, and not in parables,
We are the pieces and heaven plays the game,
We are played together in a baby-game upon the chess-
    board of existence,
And one by one we return to the box of non-existence.

Ref.: O. 94, C. 280, L. 443, B. 439, S.P. 230, P. 31, B.ii. 291, T. 183,
P. v. 10—W. 270, N. 231, E.C. 27, V. 480.

LXX.

This quatrain is translated from C. 422.

C 422.   اى رفته بچوگان قضا هبچو گو

چہ مي خور و راست برو هیچ مگو

كانكس كه ترا فگند اندر تك و دو

او داند او داند او داند او

O thou who art driven like a ball by the mallet of Fate,
Go to the right or take the left, but say nothing;[1]
For He who set thee running and galloping
He knows, he knows, he knows, he——.

Ref.: C. 422, L. 633, B. 625, P. 167, B. ii. 462, T. 274—W. 401, V. 682.

LXXI.

The origin of this quatrain is to be found in O 31.

O 31.   زين پيش نشان بودنيها بودست

پیوسته قلم ز نيك وبد ناسودست

در روز ازل هر انچه بايست بداد

غم خوردن وكوشيدن ما بيهوده ست

---

[1] This refers to the game of Polo. In the First and Second Editions for
    " Here or There " we read " Right or Left," as in the original.

LXXII.

And that inverted Bowl they call the Sky,
Whereunder crawling coop'd we live and die,
　　Lift not your hands to *It* for help—for It
As Impotently moves as you or I.

From the beginning[1] was written what shall be;
Unhaltingly the Pen (writes) and is heedless of good
    and bad;
On the First Day He appointed everything that must be—
Our grief and our efforts are vain.

Ref.: O. 31, C. 87, L. 195, B. 192, S. P. 31, B. ii. 60, T. 67, P. v. 211—
W. 35, N. 31, V. 191.

LXXII.

The inspiration for this quatrain comes from the following :

O 134 ll 1 & 2   این چرخ چو طاسیست نگون افتاده

دروی همه زیرکان زبون افتاده

This heavenly vault is like a bowl fallen upside down,
Under which all the wise have fallen helpless.

Ref.: O. 134, C. 435, L. 657, B. 649, S. P. 360, P. 34, B. ii. 481, P. v. 154
W. 408, N. 363, V. 706.

O 41.   نیکی وبدی که در نهاد بشرست

شادی وغمی که در قضا وقدرست

با چرخ مکن حواله کاندر ره عقل

چرخ از تو هزار بار بیچارهترست

The good and the bad that are in man's nature,
The happiness and misery that are predestined for us,
Do not impute them to the heavens, for, in the way of
    Wisdom,
Those heavens are a thousandfold more helpless than
    thou art.

Ref.: O. 41, C. 62, L. 80, B. 76, S.P. 95, P. 45—W. 96, N. 95, V. 79.

---

1 C. reads " Upon the Tablet."

LXXIII.

With Earth's first Clay They did the Last Man
    knead,
And there of the Last Harvest sow'd the Seed:
    And the first Morning of Creation wrote
What the Last Dawn of Reckoning shall read.

LXXIV.*

YESTERDAY *This* Day's Madness did prepare;
To-MORROW's Silence, Triumph, or Despair:
    Drink! for you know not whence you came,
        nor why:
Drink! for you know not why you go, nor where.

LXXIII.

In this quatrain we trace the influence of O. 31, (quoted in the parallel to quatrain No. 71, *ante*) and of O. 95.

O 95. ای دل چو حقیقت جهان هست مجاز

چندین چه بری خواری ازین رنج ولیاز

تن را بقضا سپار وبا وقت بساز

کین رفته قلم زبهر تو ناید باز

Oh, heart! since, in this world, truth itself is hyperbole,
Why art thou so disquieted with this trouble and abasement?
Resign thy body to destiny and adapt thyself to the times,
For, what the Pen has written, it will not re-write for thy sake.[1]

Ref.: O. 95, L. 430, B. 426, S.P. 215, P. 59, B. ii. 292.—W. 257, N. 216, E.C. 15, V. 468.

LXXIV.*

The first half of this quatrain comes from O. 152 and the second half from O. 26.

O 152. خوش باش که پخته اند سودای تو دی

ایمن شده از همه تمنای تو دی

تو شاد بزی که بی تقاضای تو دی

دادند قرار کار فردای تو دی

Be happy! they settled thy business yesterday,
And beyond the reach of all thy longings is yesterday;

---

1 Literally, "For the Pen once gone comes not back."

LXXV.

I tell you this—When, started from the Goal,
Over the flaming shoulders of the Foal
    Of Heav'n, Parwīn and Mushtarī they flung,
In my predestined Plot of Dust and Soul.

Live happily, for without any importunity on thy part
    yesterday,
They appointed with certainty what thou wilt do to-
    morrow—yesterday!

Ref.: O. 152, C. 473, L. 702, B.ii. 564, P.v. 196—W. 489, V. 754.

O 26 ll 3 & 4.   خوش باش ندانی از کجا آمده

می نوش ندانی که کجا خواهی رفت

Be happy!—thou knowest not whence thou hast come:
Drink wine!—thou knowest not whither thou shalt go.

Ref.: O. 26, C. 83, L. 192, B. 189, S.P. 85, B.ii. 110, T. 64, P.v. 34—
W. 87, N. 85, V. 188.

LXXV.

This quatrain is translated from C. 147.

C 147.   آنروز که توسن فلک زین کردند

و ارایش مشتری و پروین کردند

این بود نصیب ما ز دیوان قضا

مارا چه گنه قسمت ما این کردند

On that day when they saddled the wild horses of the
    Sun,
And settled the laws of Parwīn and Mushtarī,[1]
This was the lot decreed for me from the Diwan of Fate:
How can I sin? (my sins) are what Fate allotted me
    as my portion.

Ref.: C. 147, L. 286, B. 282, S. P. 110—W. 140, N. 110, V. 289.

----

1   See FitzGerald's note on this quatrain.

LXXVI.

The Vine had struck a fibre ; which about
If clings my Being—let the Dervish flout ;
    Of my Base metal may be filed a Key,
That shall unlock the Door he howls without.

LXXVII.

And this I know ; whether the one True Light
Kindle to Love, or Wrath-consume me quite,
    One Flash of It within the Tavern caught
Better than in the Temple lost outright.

LXXVI.

The sentiment of this quatrain is contained in C. 143.

C 143. چون بود ازل بود مرا انشا کرد

با من ز نخست درس عشق املا کرد

آنگاه قراضه ریزهٔ قلب مرا

مفتاح در خزاین معنی کرد

Since Eternity itself was He created me,
From the first he dictated to me the lesson of love,
At that time a small filing of the dust of my heart,
He made into a key of the treasure-house of substance.[1]

Ref.: C. 143, L. 311, B. 307, P. 81, T. 134,—V. 314.

LXXVII.

This quatrain is translated from O. 2.

O 2. با تو بخرابات اگر گویم راز

به زانکه بمحراب کنم بی تو نماز

ای اول و ای آخر خلقان همه تو

خواهی تو مرا بسوز وخواهی بنواز

If I talk of the mystery with Thee in a tavern,
It is better than if I make my devotions before the
Mihrab[2] without Thee.

---

1 *i.e.* of reality as opposed to the dream existence of the present. (E.B.C.)
2 The *Mihrab* is the spot in a Mosque indicating the precise direction
of Mecca towards which all Muhammadans turn in prayer.

LXXVIII.*

What ! out of senseless Nothing to provoke
A conscience Something to resent the yoke
    Of unpermitted Pleasure, under pain
Of everlasting Penalties, if broke !

O Thou, the first and last of all created beings,
Burn me an Thou wilt, or cherish me an Thou wilt.

Ref. : O. 2, C. 272, L. 427, B. 423, S. P. 221, P. 7, B. ii. 294, T. 172—
W. 262, N. 222, V. 465.

LXXVIII.*

It is not easy to deal with this and the three following
quatrains separately, the sentiments of all four being closely
interchangeable and largely identical. To avoid confusion,
however, I have attempted the task. There are some scores
of ruba'iyat that may be said to have contributed their
imageries to the quatuor. The main sources of the first of
them seem to be the following :

C 85.

یزدان چو گل وجود ما می آراست
دانست ز فعل ما چه خواهد بر خاست
بی حکمش نیست هر گناهی که مراست
پس سوختن قیامت ا بهر چه خواست

God, when he fashioned the clay of my body,
Knew by my making what would come of it ;
(Since) there is no sin of mine without his order
Why should he seek to burn me at the Day of Resur-
rection ?

Ref. : C. 85, L. 194, B. 191, S.P. 99, P. 18, T. 66—W. 100, N. 99, V. 190.

N 226.

حکیمی که از او محال باشد پرهیز
فرموده و امر کرده کز وی بگریز
انگاه میان امر و نهیش عاجز
در مانده جهانیان که کج دار و مریز

8—2

LXXIX.*

What! from his helpless Creature be repaid
Pure Gold for what he lent him dross-allay'd—
　　Sue for a Debt he never did contract,
And cannot answer—Oh the sorry trade!

Thou knowest that abstinence from that (sin) is impossible,
Having (nevertheless) ordered and ordained abstinence
from it ;
Thus between the order and the prohibition we stand
helpless,
We mortals are helpless at the permission to slant (the
cup) but not to spill (its contents).[1]

Ref. : N. 226, L. 442, B. 438, S. P. 225, P. 317, B. ii. 297, T. 180—W. 265,
V. 479.

LXXIX.*

This quatrain would seem to be specially inspired by
C. 201 and 433, which are so much alike (ll. 2, 3, and 4 are
practically identical in both) that one or the other is obviously
the addition of a later scribe.

C 201.   تا قالب خاك من بر آميخته اند
صد بو العجبي ز من بر انگيخته اند
من بهتر از اين نمى توانم بودن
كز بوته مرا چنين برون ريخته اند

When they mixed the earth of my shaping-mould,
They produced an hundred wonders from me ;[2]
I cannot be better than I am,
For this is how I was turned out of the crucible.

Ref. : C. 201, L. 355, B. 351, T. 128—W. 221, V. 354.

---

1   This metaphor recurs frequently in the ruba'iyat.   Compare W. 261,
(N. 221) and W. 275, (L. 428.)

2   *i.e.* "it was quite problematical how I might turn out."

LXXX.

Oh Thou, who didst with pitfall and with gin
Beset the Road I was to wander in,
    Thou wilt not with Predestined Evil round
Enmesh, and then impute my Fall to Sin !

LXXXI.

Oh Thou, who Man of baser Earth didst make,
And ev'n with Paradise devise the Snake :
    For all the Sin wherewith the Face of Man
Is blacken'd—Man's forgiveness give—and take !

*   *   *   *   *

LXXX.

This quatrain is translated from O. 148.

O 148. بر رهگذرم هـزار جـا دام نهی
گوئی که بگیرمت اگر گام نهی
یک ذره زحکم تو جهان خالی نیست
حکم تو کنی و عاصیم نام نهی

In a thousand places on the road I walk, Thou placest snares,

Thou say'st "I will catch thee if thou settest foot in them,"

In no smallest thing is the world independent of Thee,

Thou orderest all things, and (yet) callest me rebellious!

Ref. : O. 148, B. ii. 546—W. 432, N. 390.

LXXXI.

This is a very composite quatrain, round which some controversy has raged. Professor Cowell has given the weight of his authority to the statement that "there is no original for the line about the snake." This is true in so far as that the image does not occur in Omar, but FitzGerald had seen it in an important apologue in the Mantik ut-tair (beginning at distich 3229) in which we read of the presence of the Snake (Iblis) in Paradise, at the moment of the creation of Adam, and in the course of which, Satan himself addresses God thus:

لعنت آن تست و رحمت آن تو
بنده آن تست و قسمت آن تو
گر مرا لعنت قسمت پاک نیست
زهر هم باید همه تریاک نیست

If malediction comes from Thee, there comes also mercy,
The created thing is dependent upon Thee since Destiny
    is in Thy hands;
If malediction be my lot, I do not fear,
There must be poison, everything is not antidote.

The influence of the following is traceable in the quatrain:

C 115.   من بندهٔ عاصیم رضای تو کجاست

کاریک دلم نور و صفای تو کجاست

مرا تو بهشت اگر بطاعت بدهی

این مزد بود لطف و عطای تو کجاست

I am a disobedient slave, where is Thy mercy?
My heart is dark, where is Thy light and clearness?
If, for serving Thee, Thou givest me heaven,
This a reward, but Thy grace and Thy gifts—where
    are they?

Ref.: C. 115, L. 217, B. 214, S.P. 91, P. 23—W. 93, N. 91, V. 211.

C 286.   ای واقف اسرار ضمیر همه کس

در حالت عجز دستگیر همه کس

یارب تو مرا توبه ده و عذر پلیر

ای توبه ده و عذر پذیر همه کس

Oh! Thou who knowest the secrets of the hearts of all,
Protector of all in their hours of helplessness:
Oh, Lord! grant me repentance and accept my excuses,
Oh! Thou who grantest repentance and acceptest the
    excuses of all.

Ref.: C. 286, L. 449, B. 445, S.P. 235, B.ii. 308, T. 188—W. 276, N. 236,
V. 488.

LXXXII.

As under cover of departing Day
Slunk hunger-stricken Ramazān away,
    Once more within the Potter's house alone
I stood, surrounded by the Shapes of Clay.

LXXXIII.*

Shapes of all Sorts and Sizes, great and small,
That stood along the floor and by the wall;
    And some loquacious Vessels were; and some
Listen'd, perhaps, but never talk'd at all.

Professor Cowell attributes FitzGerald's quatrain to the above ruba'i. *Vide* the Editorial Note previously referred to.

C 510.   مازندهٔ کار مردہ و زندہ توئی

دارندهٔ این چرخ پراگندہ توئی

من گرچه بدم خواجهٔ این بندہ توئی

کسرا چه گنه نه آفریننده توئی

The manager of the affairs of the dead and living art thou,
Thou art the keeper of this unstable heaven ;
Though I am wicked, thou art my Master,
Who can sin, seeing that thou art the Creator (of all ?)

Ref.; C. 510, L. 700, B. 691, S. P. 431, P. 2, B. ii. 584.—W. 471, N. 436, V. 753.

LXXXII[1] LXXXIII* & LXXXVII (*post.*)

FitzGerald constructed these three quatrains from O. 103.

O 103.   در کارگه کوزہگری رفتم دوش

دیدم دو هزار کوزہ گویا وخموش

ناگاہ یکی کوزہ بر آورد خروش

کو کوزہگر وکوزہخر وکوزہفروش

---

1 Here begins the section devoted especially to the talking pots in the workshop of the potter—it ends at quatrain No. 90. In the first edition this section (qq. 59-66) was entitled KuzA-NAMA=the "Pot-book" or "Book of Pots." It may be observed that the quatrains in this section are not so closely rendered from recognisable originals as the other quatrains composing FitzGerald's poem. This may be accounted for by the fact that the comparison between the human form—the Personal Ego—and a pot made of earth by the Supreme Potter (if one may be allowed the phrase) is constantly recurrent in all ruba'iyat attributed to Omar Khayyam. The section is therefore to a great extent a poetical reflection upon this phase of the philosophy of the ruba'iyat. The use FitzGerald has made of O. 103 cannot fail to amaze the student. *Vide* his own Note to quatrain 89.

I went last night into the workshop of a potter,
I saw two thousand pots, some speaking, and some silent ;
Suddenly one of the pots cried out aggressively :—
" Where are the pot-maker, and the pot-buyer, and the
pot-seller ? "

Ref.: O. 103, C. 301, L. 470, B. 466, S.P. 242, P. 102, B. ii. 323, T. 202
and 297, P. v. 37.—W. 283, N. 243, E.C. 26, V. 509.

It will be observed that the reading of quatrain 87, l. 4,
in the third edition of FitzGerald is close to this original.
" Who makes—Who buys—Who sells—Who is the Pot ? "

" Hunger stricken Ramazan " is described in C. 198.

C 198. گویند که ماه رمضان گشت پدید
من بعد بگرد باده نتوان گردید
در آخر شعبان بخورم چندان مي
كاندر رمضان مست بيفتم تا عيد

They say that the moon of Ramazān[1] shines out again
Henceforth one cannot linger over the wine;
At the end of Sha'ban I will drink so much wine
That during Ramazān I may be found drunk until the
festival (arrives).

Ref.: C. 198, L. 352, B. 348, S.P. 172, P. 347, B.ii. 216, T. 125—W. 188,
N. 172, V. 351. See also the quatrain from the " Notes," p. 155.

---

1 Ramazān (or Ramadān) is the ninth month of the Muhammadan
year, which is observed as a month of fasting and penance,
during which rigid Moslems may neither eat, drink, wash, nor
caress their wives, excepting so far as is necessary to support
life. Sha'bān is the month immediately preceeding it. Shawwāl
is the month that follows it, which begins with the great feast of
Bairām, the festival referred to in line 4.

LXXXIV.

Said one among them—"Surely not in vain
" My substance of the common Earth was ta'en
        "And to this Figure moulded, to be broke,
" Or trampled back to shapeless Earth again."

LXXXV.

Then said a Second—"Ne'er a peevish Boy
" Would break the Bowl from which he drank in joy ;
        " And he that with his hand the Vessel made
" Will surely not in after Wrath destroy."

,

LXXXIV.

The sentiment of this quatrain is traceable in C. 293.

جامیست که عقل آفرین می زلدش   C 293.

صد بوسه ز حسن بر جبین می زلدش

این کوزه گر دهر چنین جام لطیف

میسازد و باز بر زمین می زلدش

There is a cup which wisdom loud acclaims,
And for its beauty gives it a hundred kisses on the brow,
Such a sweet cup, this Potter of the World
Makes, and then shatters it upon the ground.

Ref.: C. 293, L. 456, B. 452, B. ii. 321, T. 194—W. 290, V. 495.

LXXXV.

The inspiration for this quatrain comes from O. 19.

لرکیب پیاله که در می پیوست   O 19.

بشکستن آن روا لمی دارد مست

چندین سر و پای نازنین ازسر دست

از مهر که پیوست وبکین که شکست

The elements of a cup which he has put together,
Their breaking up a drinker cannot approve;[1]
All these heads and feet—with his finger-tips,
For love of whom did he make them ?—for hate of whom
      did he break them ?

Ref.: O. 19, C. 64, L. 40, S. P. 37, P. ii. 7, P. 95, B. ii. 77, T. 309—
W. 42, N. 38, V. 220.

---

1 A very obscure distich to translate. The sense is here, however.

LXXXVI.

After a momentary silence spake
Some Vessel of a more ungainly make ;
    "They sneer at me for leaning all awry :
"What! did the Hand then of the Potter shake ? "

LXXXVII.

Whereat some one of the loquacious Lot—
I think a Súfi pipkin—waxing hot—
    "All this of Pot and Potter—Tell me, then,
"Who is the Potter, pray, and who the Pot ? "

LXXXVIII.

" Why," said another, "Some there are who tell
"Of one who threatens he will toss to Hell
    "The luckless Pots he marr'd in making—Pish !
" He's a Good Fellow, and 'twill all be well."

LXXXVI.

This quatrain is a perfect reflection and companion of all these Kūza Nāma quatrains, but I have not found a ruba'i in O. or C. which can be pointed out as having directly inspired[1] it. It must, I think, be considered together with No. 88.

LXXXVII. *Ante sub* LXXXIII.

LXXXVIII.

The inspiration for this quatrain, and I think for No. 86, comes from the following :

C 69. دارنده چو ترکیب طبائع آراست

باز از چه سبب فگندش اندر کم و کاست

گر نیك آمد شکستنش از بهر چه بود

ور بد آمد پس این صور عیب چراست

Since the Director set in order the elements of natures,
For what cause does He again disperse them into loss and deficiency ?
If they are good, why should He break them ?
And if they turn out bad, well, why is there any blame to these forms ?

---

1 Compare Romans ch. ix. v. 21. " Hath not the potter power over the clay, of the same lump to make one vessel unto honour, and another unto dishonour ? "

LXXXIX.

" Well," murmured one, " Let whoso make or buy,
" My Clay with long Oblivion is gone dry:
    " But fill me with the old familiar Juice,
" Methinks I might recover by and by."

Ref.: C. 69, L. 103, B. 99, P. 94, B. ii. 107—W. 126, V. 103.

C 159.
گویند بمشر جستجو خواهد بود
و ان یارعزیز تندخو خواهد بود
ازخیر محض جز نکوئی ناید هرگز
خوش باش که عاقبت نکو خواهد بود

They say that at the resurrection there will be much
    searching,
And that that excellent Friend will be hasty;
Nothing but good ever came from the Unalloyed Good-
    ness,
Be happy! for the upshot will be all right!

Ref.: C. 159, L. 316, B. 312, S.P. 178, P. 197—W. 193, N. 178, V. 318.

———

LXXXIX.

This quatrain is inspired by the following:

C 188
آندم که نهال عمر من کنده شود
و اجرام ز یکدگر پر اگنده شود
گر زانکه صراحی کنند از گل من
حالی که پر از باده کند زنده شود

At that moment when the plant of my existence shall
        be rooted up,
And its branches scattered in all directions;
If then they make a flagon of my clay,
When they fill it with wine it will live again.

XC.

So while the Vessels one by one were speaking,
The little Moon look'd in that all were seeking:
 And then they jogg'd each other, " Brother!
 Brother!
" Now for the Porter's shoulder-knot a-creaking! "

     *   *   *   *

Ref.: C. 188, S.P. 115—N. 115.

O 116.

در پای اجل چو من سرافگنده شوم

وز بیخ امید عمر بر کنده شوم

زنهار گلم بجز صراحی مکنید

شاید که چو پر باده شود زنده شوم

When I am abased beneath the foot of Destiny,
And am rooted up from the hope of life,
Take heed that thou makest nothing but a goblet of my
    clay,
Haply when it is full of wine I may revive.

Ref.: O. 116, C. 345, L. 539, B. 534, S.P. 289, P. 227, B. ii. 385, T. 230,
P. v. 146.—W. 330, N. 290, V. 579.

—————

XC.

This quatrain which concludes the Kūza Nāmeh is inspired by the concluding quatrain of O. (158.)

O 158.

ماه رمضان برفت وشوال آمد

هنگام نشاط عیش وقوال آمد

آمد که آنکه خیکها اندر دوش

گویند که پشت پشت حمال آمد

The month of Ramazān passes and Shawwāl comes,[1]
The season of increase, and joy, and storytellers comes;
Now comes that time when " Bottles upon the shoulder!"
They say—for the porters come and are back to back.[2]

Ref.: O. 158—W. 218.

———————————

1 See note 1 on page 125.

2 *i.e.* Helping one another to raise their loads. Prof. Denison Ross
suggests that this refers to the cry of the porters and muleteers in the
narrow streets of Persian cities. "*Pusht! Pusht!*" *i.e.* " Mind your
backs!"

XCI.

Ah, with the Grape my fading life provide,
And wash thé Body whence the Life has died,
    And lay me, shrouded in the living Leaf,
By some not unfrequented Garden-side.

XCI.

This quatrain owes its inspiration to C. 12.

C 12.

چون فوت شوم ببادہ شوئید مرا
تلقین ز شراب ناب گوئید مرا
خواهی کہ بروز حشر بینید مرا
از خاك در میكدہ جوئید مرا

When I am dead wash me with wine,
Say my funeral service with pure wine,
If thou wishest that thou shouldst see me on the resurrec-
tion-day
Thou must seek me in the earth of the tavern threshold.

Ref.: C. 12, L. 13, B. 12, S.P. 7, P. 299, B. ii. 9, T. 12—W. 6, N. 7, V. 11.

O. 69 may also be quoted:

O 69.

زنهار مرا زجــام مـي قوت کنید
وین چهرہ کهربا چو یاقوت کنید
چون در گذرم بمی بشوئید مـرا
وز چوب رزم تخته تابوت کنید

Take heed to stay me with the wine-cup,
And make this amber[1] face like a ruby;
When I die, wash me with wine,
And out of the wood of the vine, make the planks of
my coffin.

Ref.: O. 69, C. 158, L. 308, B. 304, S.P. 109, P. 212, B. ii. 199, T. 143,
P.v. 153—W. 139, N. 109, V. 311.

---

1 *Kah-ruba* means literally "attracting straws;" hence "amber," the
ἤλεκτρον of the Greeks. Here it is used in the descriptive sense
to mean "yellow." *See* note 2 on p. 15.

XCII.

That ev'n my buried Ashes such a snare
Of Vintage shall fling up into the Air
    As not a True-believer passing by
But shall be overtaken unaware.

XCIII.

Indeed the Idols I have loved so long
Have done my credit in this World much wrong:
    Have drown'd my Glory in a shallow Cup,
And sold my Reputation for a Song.

XCII.

This quatrain is translated from C. 16.

C 16.   چندان بخورم شراب کین بوی شراب

آید ز تراب چون شوم زیر تراب

تا بر سر خاک من رسد مخموری

از بوی شراب من شود مست و خراب

I will drink so much wine that this aroma of wine
Shall rise from the earth when I am beneath it;
So that when a drinker shall pass above my body,
He shall become drunk and degraded from the aroma
of my potations.

Ref.: C. 16, L. 28, B. 26, S.P. 14, B.ii. 11—W. 17, N. 14, V. 27.

XCIII.

The inspiration for this quatrain comes from the following:

C 170.   طبعم بنماز و روزه چون مائل شد

گفتم که نهایت کلیم حاصل شد

افسوس کهآن وضو بباری بشکست

و آن روزه به نیم جرعه می باطل شد

When my mood inclined to prayer and fasting,
I said that all my salvation was attained;
Alas! that those Ablutions[1] are destroyed by my
pleasures,

---

1 *Wuzu*, the ceremonial Ablution enjoined upon Muhammadans to put
them into a state of grace before prayer.

XCIV.

Indeed, indeed, Repentance oft before
I swore—but was I sober when I swore?
    And then and then came Spring, and Rose-in-
        hand
My thread-bare Penitence apieces tore.

XCV.

And much as Wine has play'd the Infidel,
And robb'd me of my Robe of Honour—Well,
    I wonder often what the Vintners buy
One half so precious as the stuff they sell.

And that Fast of mine is annulled by half a draught of
wine.

Ref.: C. 170, L. 366, B. 362, S.P. 162, P. 343, B.ii. 207, T. 118—W. 180,
N. 162, V. 365.

The last line is suggested by O. 22, *q.v. post* p. 149.

XCIV.

This quatrain is inspired by C. 431.

C 431.   هر روز بر آنم که کنم شب توبه
از جام و پیالهٔ لبالب توبه
اکنون که رسید وقت گل هرگم نیست
در موسم گل ز توبه یا رب توبه

Every day I resolve to repent in the evening,
Making repentance of the brimful goblet and cup;
Now that the season of roses[1] has come, I cannot grieve
Give penitence for repentance in the season of roses,
    O Lord !

Ref.: C. 431, L. 655, B. 647, B. ii. 510—W. 425, V. 704.

XCV.

The original of this quatrain is O. 62.

O 62.   با آنکه شراب پردهٔ ما بدرید
تا جان دارم نخواهم از باده برید
من در عجبم زمی فروشان کایشان
به زین که فروشند چه خواهند خرید

---

1   *Wakt-i-gul* = the season of roses, a common synonym for Spring.

XCVI.

Yet Ah, that Spring should vanish with the Rose!
That Youth's sweet-scented manuscript should close!
    The Nightingale that in the branches sang,
Ah whence, and whither flown again, who knows!

XCVII.*

Would but the Desert of the Fountain yield
One glimpse—if dimly, yet indeed, reveal'd,
    To which the fainting Traveller might spring,
As springs the trampled herbage of the field!

Although wine has rent my veil (of reputation),
So long as I have a soul I will not be separated from
    wine;
I am in perplexity concerning vintners, for they—
What will they buy that is better than what they sell?

Ref.: O. 62, C. 196, L. 350, B. 346, P. 311, B. ii. 167, T. 123, P. iv. 63,
P. v. 202.—W. 208, N. 463, E.C. 11, V. 350.

XCVI.

This quatrain is translated from C. 223.

C 233.
افسوس که نامهٔ جوانی طی شد
وین تازه بهار ارغوانی دی شد
آن مرغ طرب که نام او بود شباب
افسوس ندالم که کی آمد کی شد

Alas! that the book of youth is folded up?
And that this fresh purple spring is winter-stricken;[1]
That bird of joy, whose name is Youth,
Alas! I know not when it came nor when it went.

Ref.: C. 223, L. 332, B. 328, S.P. 128, B. ii. 155, T. 161.—W. 155, N. 128
V. 334.

XCVII.*

This quatrain is inspired by C. 509.

C 509.
ای کاش که جائی آرمیدن بودی
یا این رهرا بسر رسیدن بودی
کاش از پی صد هزار سال از دل خاك
چون سبزه امید بر دمیدن بودی

---

[1] Literally "has become Dai," the first winter-month; translated
"December," *sub* quatrain No. 9. *Vide* note 1 p. 21.

XCVIII.*

Would but some wingéd Angel ere too late
Arrest the yet unfolded Roll of Fate,
     And make the stern Recorder otherwise
Enregister, or quite obliterate!

Oh! would that there were a place of repose,
Or that we might come to the end of the road;
Would that from the heart of earth, after a hundred
thousand years,
We might all hope to blossom again like the verdure.

Ref.: C. 509, L. 768, B. 754, S. P. 395, B. ii. 522—W. 442, N. 400,
V. 820.

XCVIII.*

This quatrain in its original form in the second edition
was closer to the original Persian. It owes its inspiration
to N. 457.

Oh if the World were but to re-create,
That we might catch ere closed the Book of Fate,
And make the Writer on a fairer leaf
Inscribe our names, or quite obliterate!

N 457.   يزدان خواهم جهان دگر گون كندي
و اكنوي كندي تا نگرم چون كندي
يا نام من از جريده بيرون كندي
يا روزي من ز غيب افزون كندي

I would that God should entirely alter the world,
And that he should do it now, that I might see him do it;
And either that he should cross my name from the Roll,
Or else raise my condition from want to plenty.[1]

Ref.: N. 457, S. P. 451—W. 486, V. 841.

----

1 *Lit.*: "Or from the invisible world increase my daily provision."

XCIX.

Ah, Love! could you and I with Him conspire
To grasp this sorry Scheme of Things entire,
　　Would not we shatter it to bits—and then
Re-mould it nearer to the Heart's Desire!

　　*　　*　　*　　*　　*　　*

C.

Yon rising moon that looks for us again—
How oft hereafter will she wax and wane;
　　How oft hereafter rising look for us
Through this same Garden—and for *one* in vain.

XCIX.

This quatrain is translated from C. 395.

C 395. گر بر فلکم دست بودی چون یزدان

بر داشتمی من این فلک را ز میان

از نو فلکی دگر چنان ساختمی

کازاده بکام دل رسیدی آسان

Had I, like God, control of the heavens,
Would I not do away with the heavens altogether,
Would I not so construct another heaven from the be-
    ginning
That, being free, one might attain to the heart's desire?

Ref.: C. 395, L. 594, B. 587, S. P. 337, P. 98, B. ii. 450, T. 268—W. 379,
N. 340, V. 641.

C.

This quatrain in its various forms is inspired by O. 5.

O 5. چون عهده نمی کند کسی فردارا

حالی خوش کن تو این دل شیدارا

می نوش بنور ماه ای ماه که ماه

بسیار بجوید و نیابد مارا

Since no one will guarantee thee a to-morrow,
Make thou happy now this lovesick heart; [1]
Drink wine in the moonlight, O Moon, for the moon [2]
Shall seek us long and shall not find us.

---

1 C. reads " this heart full of melancholy (or passion)."
2 It will be observed that this quatrain in the first edition came a good
    deal closer to the original than this.

CI.

And when like her, oh Sākī, you shall pass
Among the Guests Star-scatter'd on the Grass,
  And in your joyous errand reach the spot
Where I made One—turn down an empty Glass!

Ref. : O. 5, C. 7, L. 5, S.P. 8, P. 219, B. 4, B. ii. 8, T. 6, P. v. 168.—W. 7, N. 8, E.C. 5, V. 4.

CI.

This quatrain is taken from O. 83 and 84.

O 83.

یاران چو باتفاق دیدار کنید

باید که ز دوست یاد بسیار کنید

چون بادهٔ خوشگوار نوشید بهم

نوبت چو بما رسد نگونسار کنید

Friends when ye hold a meeting together,
It behoves ye warmly to remember your friend;
When ye drink wholesome wine together,
And my turn comes, turn (a goblet) upside down.

Ref.: O. 83—W. 234, V. 459.

O 84.

یاران بموافقت چو میعاد کنید

خودرا بجمال یکدگر شاد کنید

ساقی چو می مغانه بر کف گیرد

بیچاره فلانرا بدعا یاد کنید

Friends, when with consent ye make a tryst together,
And take delight in one another's charms,
When the Cup-bearer takes (round) in his hand the
    Mugh[1] wine,
Remember a certain helpless one in your benediction.

Ref.: O. 84, L. 290, B. 286, S.P. 191, P. 226, B.ii. 245—W. 205, N. 192, V. 293.

---

1 *Mughanah* means anything connected with the Mughs or Magians, (*i.e.*, the Guebres or Fire-worshippers), and came to be a synonym for age, superiority, excellence, in which sense it is used here. S. Rousseau has a very interesting note upon the history of this word at p. 176 of his "Flowers of Persian Literature" (London, 1801).

Int. p. 8.

Khayyām, who stitched the Tents of Science,
Has fallen in Grief's furnace and been suddenly burned ;
The shears of Fate have cut the tent-ropes of his life,
And the Broker of Hope has sold him for nothing !

APPENDIX.

In addition to the quatrains composing the final form in which we know his poem, there are a few stray quatrains scattered about Edward FitzGerald's Introduction and Notes. There are also two quatrains which appeared in the first edition only, and nine that appeared in the second edition only. I do not think that this work would be complete without an attempt to identify these quatrains in the original texts which inspired them.

In the Introduction.

The quatrain upon p. 8 is a literal translation by Prof. Cowell of O. 22.

O 22. خیّام که خیمهای حکمت می‌دوخت
در کورهٔ غم فتاد و ناگاه بسوخت
مقراض اجل طناب عمرش برید
دلّال امل برایگانش بفروخت

Ref.: O. 22, C. 59, L. 74, B. 70, S. P. 81, P. 205, B. ii. 94, T. 307, P. iv. 65, P. v. 195—W. 83, N. 81, V. 73.

The quatrain upon p. 14 is FitzGerald's rendering of C. 1.

C 1. ای سوخته سوخته سوختنی
وای که آتش دوزخ از تو افروختنی

Int. p. 14.

Oh, Thou who burn'st in Heart for those who burn
In Hell, whose fires thyself shall feed in turn;
    How long be crying, "Mercy on them, God!"
Why, who art Thou to teach, and He to learn?

Int. p. 15.

If I myself upon a looser Creed
Have loosely strung the Jewel of Good deed,
Let this one thing for my Atonement plead,
That One for Two I never did misread.

تا کی گولی که بر عمر رحمت کن

حق را تو کجای رحمت اموختنی

O, burnt one (born) of the burnt ! destined in turn to burn,
And oh, thou! from whom the fires of Hell shall blaze,[1]
How long wilt thou keep saying, "Have mercy upon
    Omar ! "
Wilt *thou* be a teacher of mercy to *God?*

Ref.: C. 1, L. 769, B. 755, S. P. 453, P. ii. 1, B. ii. 537, T. 1—W. 488,
N. 459, V. 821.

The quatrain on p. 15 is FitzGerald's rendering of O. 1.

O 1. گر گوهر طاعت نسفتم هرگز

گرد گنه از چهره نرفتم هرگز

با این همه نومید لیم از کرمت

زان رو که یکیرا دو نگفتم هرگز

If I have never threaded the pearl[2] of thy service,
And if I have never wiped the dust of sin from my face,
Nevertheless, I am not hopeless of thy mercy,
For the reason that I have never said that One was Two.[3]

Ref. : O. 1, C. 274, L. 423, B. 419, P. 4, S. P. 228, B. ii. 302, P. iv. 8—
W. 268, N. 229, V. 461.

---

1 Prof. Cowell says : " I am not sure, but I fancy this hard verse really
    is: " O thou who art burned (in sorrow) for one burnt (in hell)—
    thyself being doomed to be burnt." If this is correct, (which is
    most probable) the accuracy of FitzGerald's translation is re-
    markable.

2 The phrase *gauhar suftan* = " to thread pearls " is used in Persian to
    mean " to write verses " or " to tell a story." Omar uses it here
    referring to the generally antinomian tendency of his ruba'iyat.

3 In this line Omar claims consideration on the ground that he has
    never questioned the Unity of God. *Tawhid kerdan*=to acknow-
    ledge One God. Muhammadanism is essentially Unitarian. Fitz-
    Gerald appears to have missed the meaning here, reversing the
    doctrine, unless he means " I never misread One *as* Two."

Note xviii.

The Palace that to Heav'n his pillars threw,
And Kings the forehead on his threshold drew—
   I saw the solitary Ringdove there,
And "Coo, coo, coo!" she cried, and "Coo, coo,
     coo."

IN THE NOTES.

The quatrain in the note to quatrain No. 18 is translated from C. 419.

C 419. آن قصر که با چرخ همي زد پهلو

بر درگه او شهان نهادندي رو

دیدیم که بر کنگرہ اش فاخته

آواز همي داد که کو کو کو کو

That palace that reared its pillars up to heaven,
Kings prostrated themselves upon its threshold;
I saw a dove that, upon its battlements,
Uttered its cry: "Where, where, where, where?"[1]

Ref.: C. 419, L. 627, B. 619, S.P. 347, P. 140, B.ii. 459, P.iv. 13—W. 392, N. 350, V. 677.

The quatrain in the note to quatrain No. 90 is translated from C. 218.

C 218. خوش باش که ماہ عید تو خواهد شد

اسباب طرب جمله نکو خواهد شد

مہ زرد و خمیدہ قد و لاغر شدہ اسـت

گوئي که درین رنج فرو خواهد شد

---

1 L. 1. *lit.* "rubbed its side with heaven." This is the quatrain that R. B. M. Binning found written upon a stone in the ruins of Persepolis (A Journal of Two Years Travel in Persia, Ceylon, etc., London, 1857, Vol. ii. p. 20). FitzGerald quotes it in a letter to Prof. Cowell, under date 13th January, 1859. (Letters and Literary Remains of Edward FitzGerald, London, 1889. Macmillan, 3 vols., and 1894, 2 vols.) The word *ku* in Persian signifies "Where?"

Note xc.

Be of Good Cheer—the sullen Month will die,
And a young Moon requite us by and by :
    Look how the Old one, meagre, bent, and wan
With Age and Fast, is fainting from the Sky!

Edit. I.—xxxiii.

Then to the rolling Heav'n itself I cried,
Asking, "What Lamp had Destiny to guide
    " Her little Children stumbling in the Dark?"
And—"A blind Understanding!" Heav'n replied.

Edit. I.—xlv.

But leave the Wise to wrangle, and with me
The quarrel of the Universe let be ;
    And, in some corner of the Hubbub coucht,
Make Game of that which makes as much of Thee.

Edit. I.—xxxvii.

Ah! fill the Cup—what boots it to repeat
How Time is slipping underneath our Feet ?
    Unborn To-morrow and dead Yesterday.
Why fret about them if To-day be sweet ?

Be happy! for the moon of thy festival will come,[1]
The means of mirth will all be propitious ;
This moon has become lean, bent-figured and thin,
Thou may'st say that it will sink under this trouble.

Ref.: C. 218, B. ii. 186.

IN THE FIRST EDITION.

In the first edition we find quatrain No. 33, which, like its distant cousin in the fourth edition (No. 34), appears to have no near parallel in the texts. No. 45 is a quatrain in a like predicament, and it may be for this reason that Fitz-Gerald dropped it out of all subsequent editions.

The only other quatrain peculiar to the first edition is No. 37. This would appear to have been inspired by ll. 3 and 4 of O. 20, quoted in the parallels to quatrain No. 57 and by O. 17, ll. 3 and 4.

O 17 ll 3 & 4. از دي كه گذشت هر چه گوئي خوش نيست

خوش باش و ز دي مگو كه امروز خوشست

Nothing thou canst say of yesterday, that is past, is sweet;
Be happy and do not speak of yesterday, for to-day is sweet.

Ref.: O. 17, C. 84, L. 193, B. 190, P. 126, B. ii. 59, T. 65 and 352, P. iv. 68, P. v. 62—W. 112, E. C. 6, V. 189.

IN THE SECOND EDITION.

The quatrains peculiar to the second edition are as follows:

---

1 See note on page 125.

Edit. II.—xiv.

' Were it not Folly, Spider-like to spin
The Thread of present Life away to win—
    What ? for ourselves, who know not if we shall
Breathe out the very Breath we now breathe in!

Edit. II.—xliv.

Do you, within your little hour of Grace,
The waving Cypress in your Arms enlace,
    Before the Mother back into her arms
Fold, and dissolve you in a last embrace.

XIV.

This quatrain is inspired by O. 136.

O 136. تاكي غم آن خورم كه دارم يانه

وين عمر بخوش دلي گذارم يانه

پر كن قدح باده كه معلومم نيست

كين دم كه فرو برم برآرام يانه

How long shall I grieve about what I have or have not,
And whether I shall pass this life light-heartedly or not?
Fill up the wine-cup, for I do not know
That I shall breathe out the breath that I am drawing
in.

Ref.: O. 136, C. 504 and 427, L. 740, B. 726, S.P. 362, P. 207, B.ii. 484,
P.v. 64—W. 411, N. 366, V. 730.

XXVIII.

This was replaced by No. 63 in the fourth edition taken
from the same original.

XLIV.

The sentiment of this quatrain is traceable in the
following :

C 189 ll 1 & 2. شاديها كن كه آلزمان خواهد بود

جسم همه در خاك نهان خواهد بود

Be happy ! for the time will come
(When) all bodies will be hidden in the earth.

Ref.: C. 189, L. 393, B. 389, S.P. 160, B. ii. 203.—N. 160, V. 390.

Edit. II.—lxv.

If but the Vine and Love-abjuring Band
Are in the Prophet's Paradise to stand,
       Alack, I doubt the Prophet's Paradise
Were empty as the hollow of one's Hand.

C 195. طبعم همه با روي چو گل پیوندد

دستم همه با ساغر مل پیوندد

از هر جزوي نصیب خود بر دارم

زان پیش که جز وها بکل پیوندد

My whole mood is in sympathy with rosy cheeks,
My hand is always grasping the wine cup ;
I exact from every part (of me) its allotted function,
Ere that those parts (of me) be mingled with the all.

Ref.: C. 195, L. 349, B. 345, S.P. 163, P. 287, B. ii. 206, T. 122.—W. 181, N. 163, V. 349.

LXV.

This quatrain is inspired by the following :—

O 127. می خوردن و گرد نیکوان گردیدن

به زانك بزرق زاهدی ورزیدن

گر عاشق ومست دوزخي خواهد بود

پس روي بهشت کس نخواهد دیدن

To drink wine and consort with a company of the
    beautiful
Is better than practising the hypocrisy of the zealot ;
If the lover and the drunkard are doomed to hell,
Then no one will see the face of heaven.

Ref.: O. 127, L. 608, B. 601, S.P. 339, P. 330, B.ii. 453, P.v. 151—W. 381, N. 342, V. 655.

Edit. II.—lxxvii.

For let Philosopher and Doctor preach
Of what they will, and what they will not,—each
　　　Is but one Link in an eternal Chain
That none can slip, nor break, nor over-reach.

Edit. II.—lxxxvi.

Nay, but, for terror of his wrathful Face,
I swear I will not call Injustice Grace;
　　　Not one Good Fellow of the Tavern but
Would kick so poor a Coward from the place.

FitzGerald was evidently "reminded of" this by N. 64 which is C. 60.

C 60.   گویند که دوزخي بود مردم مست

قولیست خلاف دل درو نتوان بست

گر عاشق مست دوزخي خواهد بود

فردا بیني بهشت را چون کف دست

They say that drunkards will go to hell,
It is a repugnant creed, the heart cannot believe it ;
If drunken lovers are doomed to hell,
To-morrow heaven will be bare like the palm of one's
    hand.

Ref.: C. 60, L. 158, B. 155, S.P. 64, T. 308, P.v. 29—W. 67, N. 64,
V. 156.

LXXVII.

For this quatrain I can find neither authority nor inspiration.

LXXXVI.

I think the inspiration for this must have been C. 8.

C 8.   مرد آن نبود که خلق خارند اورا

وز بیم بدي لیك شمارند اورا

رندي که نبود پست دستي بکرم

رندان همه پست دست دارند اورا

No man is he whom his fellow men spurn,
And (at the same time) for fear of his malice number
    among the good ;

Edit. II.—xc.

And once again there gather'd a scarce heard
Whisper among them; as it were, the stirr'd
    Ashes of some all but extinguisht Tongue,
Which mine ear kindled into living Word.

Edit. II.—xcix.

Whither resorting from the vernal Heat
Shall Old Acquaintance Old Acquaintance greet,
    Under the Branch that leans above the Wall
To shed his Blossom over head and feet.

Edit. II.—cvii.

Better, oh better, cancel from the Scroll
Of Universe one luckless Human Soul,
    Than drop by drop enlarge the Flood that rolls
Hoarser with Anguish as the Ages roll.

If a drunkard shows reluctance in generosity,
All his fellow drunkards hold him to be a mean fellow.

Ref.: C. 8, L. 3, B. ii. 15, T. 9—V. 416.

XC.

This was a fourth quatrain evolved out of O. 103. *Vide* quatrain Nos. 82, 83 and 87 *ante.*

XCIX.

This quatrain, interpolated after No. 91 of the fourth edition, (= No. 98 of the second edition) is an elaboration founded upon the story told by Nizam ul-Mulk and recorded by FitzGerald in his introduction (p. 9).

CVII.

This quatrain, interpolated after the quatrain which became No. xcviii. in the fourth edition, was no doubt inspired by N. 457 (*q.v. sub* No. 98 *ante*) and by O. 54.

O 54. از رفته قلم هیچ دگر گون نشود
وزخوردن غم بجزجگر خون نشود
کر در همه عمر خویش خولابه خوری
یك قطره ازآن که هست افزون نشود

What the Pen has written never changes,
And grieving only results in deep affliction;
Even through all thy life thou weepest tears of blood,
Not one drop becomes increased beyond what it is.

Ref.: O. 54, B.ii. 144.

تمام شد

www.ingramcontent.com/pod-product-compliance
Lightning Source LLC
Chambersburg PA
CBHW020000030726
47500CB00002B/365